Sequence

The middle-aged son of a matriarchal family has been reported missing. DCI Ian Roper returns from a weekend visit to his son to learn that Brenda Gibbons, one of his detective constables, is making tentative inquiries into the disappearance: tentative because Bruce Selby is not considered to be vulnerable and has no criminal record, although there seems to be no obvious reason for him to abandon his comfortable existence at home.

Meanwhile other officers are following up a spate of arson attacks on property and a PC is making inquiries concerning seemingly random acts of vandalism directed at an elderly lady who lives alone.

When a body is discovered it ties in neatly with the disappearance of Bruce Selby but there is also the possibility that someone else has gone missing which leads the investigation to a recently opened gay bar and several individuals who are in some way connected with local planning.

The past lives of these characters are examined closely and a link is found between them all, one which turns out to lead to a false trail. One by one the suspects are eliminated. Only when the motive for the crime becomes apparent is DCI Roper able to make an arrest.

An ingenious plot provides nail-biting suspense and a satisfying denouement in this popular crime writer's sixth whodunit.

Also by Janie Bolitho

Kindness can kill (1993)
Ripe for revenge (1994)
Motive for murder (1994)
Dangerous deceit (1995)
Finger of fate (1996)

SEQUENCE OF SHAME

Janie Bolitho

Constable · London

First published in Great Britain 1996
by Constable & Company Ltd
3 The Lanchesters, 162 Fulham Palace Road
London W6 9ER
Copyright © 1996 by Janie Bolitho
The right of Janie Bolitho to be
identified as the author of this work
has been asserted by her in accordance with
the Copyright, Designs and Patents Act 1988
ISBN 0 09 476500 6
Set in Palatino 10pt by
Pure Tech India Ltd, Pondicherry
Printed and bound in Great Britain by
Hartnolls Ltd, Bodmin, Cornwall

A CIP catalogue record for this book
is available from the British Library

For my mother, Pam Tunley

Acknowledgements to Julian Bolitho
Environment and Development Dept. Leicester

1

Theo Selby had been dead for seven years. An organised, careful man, he left behind him a large house, fully paid for, legacies and insurance policies and the extended family with whom he had lived and who continued to remain under the same roof. Only his wife, Elizabeth, was aware of the circumstances which had caused her shame and embarrassment many years previously.

Breakfast in the Selby household was still eaten in the conservatory amongst the potted plants but wholemeal toast and Kellogg's cornflakes had long since replaced the traditional kidneys and kedgeree. Maurice, Elizabeth's older son, was already seated, as was his wife, Norma, and their own two children.

'No Bruce?' Elizabeth inquired as she poured coffee. It was Friday morning and there were things she wished to discuss with her second son.

'No.' Maurice spread marmalade on his toast. 'And the bolts weren't across when I brought in the milk.'

Elizabeth was certain then that he had not returned home the previous night but she went up to his room to make sure. He was not there. She returned to the conservatory with her usual composed expression. If she was unduly concerned the rest of the family did not see it. Bruce occasionally spent a night away from home but was always courteous enough to inform her in advance. He would return at some point, of that she was sure.

Elizabeth Selby sipped her coffee and poured a second cup. She was not hungry. Studying Maurice, her favourite son, now engrossed in the paper, she saw that his ginger hair was thinning and his shirt buttons strained across his chest, but his humour and ability to entertain made up for anything he might lack in looks. She wondered if it would be tactful to suggest he bought some larger shirts or wore a vest because fatty tissue, like undeveloped breasts, and the dark circles of his nipples were visible through the white cotton. No, it was better to leave that sort of thing to Norma. Dear Norma; intelligent, witty and beautiful, all she had ever hoped for in a daughter-in-law, and as even-tempered as Maurice. The children had never caused any anxiety either and were now at the stage where they spent most of their time with friends.

'A lady, do you think?' Maurice grinned over the top of the newspaper.

'Pardon?' Elizabeth had been deep in thought.

'Brucie. That's two nights he's not come home. Do you suppose he's found a woman at last?'

Elizabeth shrugged non-committally. There surely had been some but Bruce refused to bring them home. He was no youngster, it was time he was married and preferably to someone quite a few years his junior because at forty-three he was leaving it rather late to start a family.

Breakfast over, everyone departed to their various destinations. Elizabeth did not move until the daily help came in to clear the table. She went upstairs to the master-bedroom which she had retained since Theo's death because it was spacious, large enough to double as a sitting-room, a sanctuary when Maurice and Norma had guests or she needed a break from the children. The bed was already made and sunlight streamed in through the open balcony windows. The air was still and sultry but the promised summer storms had not come. Sitting at a small table she thought back over the previous day.

Bruce had not been at breakfast then either, but he had not been expected. He had telephoned on Wednesday to say he was staying overnight with a friend.

'May I know her name?' Elizabeth had inquired.

'Not just yet. When you meet her.' Bruce had sounded smug. She was pleased, this time it might be serious, this time he might really bring a woman home.

The day had passed uneventfully but the heat left Elizabeth feeling lethargic so she did no more than sit in the garden in the shade and read. In the evening she had taken a chicken salad to her room and eaten it at the table where she now sat. No one else was in and Thursday was the night the local council met. Bruce, being a member, should have been there. Elizabeth's memory was sharp and accurate. She recalled how her hand had hovered over the salt cellar until she had decided that doctors were no longer able to make up their minds what was or was not good for you. She had shaken a generous portion on to her plate feeling virtuous that the salad cream was low-fat. Relaxed and enjoying an evening of solitude she had watched the cows, tails flicking, in a distant field and wondered why shop tomatoes did not taste the same as the ones Theo used to grow.

The telephone had rung and disturbed her reverie. Automatically she had glanced at her dainty gold wrist-watch. She had expected the call to be for one of the children, who received the majority lately. The silk dress had rustled pleasantly against her lean body as she crossed the room to pick up the extension beside her bed.

'No,' she had said in response to a question. 'No, I'm sorry, I've no idea.' When she replaced the receiver anxiety had gripped her and something Bruce had told her came to mind. Unable to eat she had come to a decision. She had to know, for her own peace of mind.

But that was yesterday, Thursday, and now it was getting on for midday on Friday and there was still no word from Bruce. And it was not as if she could ring him at work, his office adjoined his bedroom, two doors down the landing from her own.

The oppressive weather, combined with worry, felt like a physical weight pressing down on her head. At one thirty she telephoned Maurice but Bruce had not been in touch with him.

The afternoon dragged slowly to an end and, one by one, the

7

other members of the family returned. They waited until eight to eat dinner. It was a quiet affair, Elizabeth's mood was affecting them all.

'Look,' Maurice said suddenly, putting down his knife and fork. 'I think we ought to do something. I mean, this just isn't like Bruce.'

'He's right,' Norma added, her pale face concerned.

'Such as what?' Elizabeth already knew the answer.

'I think we should contact the police.'

'Yes, Maurice, I think we'll have to.' There was, she realised, no alternative.

Everyone who was *au fait* with the drinking establishments in Rickenham Green, and many who were not, knew that the Prince William in Buckton Road had been closed for two months for renovation and much-needed redecoration. The reopening was eagerly awaited: rumour had it that it was to become a gay bar. Rumour, for once, was right and on the first night it was packed, people standing elbow to elbow because a large write-up in the *Rickenham Herald* had announced there would be live music and a free buffet. But these inducements did not compete with blatant curiosity.

Gone was the filthy carpet, the pool table and the gaming machines; gone were the plastic-covered bench seats and the rickety tables with their cigarette burns. Instead there was a thick-piled carpet, individual tables of polished wood designed to seat no more than four, a mahogany bar which was new as were all the fixtures and fittings. There were jugs of flowers and a stack of gay newspapers on the windowsill.

Everyone prophesied failure, they said that there was not a large enough clientele in Rickenham and surrounding areas. Everyone was wrong. Initially the curiosity value attracted heterosexual couples and groups of girls on a night out but many continued to use the place once they saw how clean it was and that there was nothing to shock or offend them. Sebastian

Roberts had purchased the premises from the brewery, he had to make it work. He introduced food and his menu was so varied that several other pubs had to revamp their own as the lunchtime trade from the Town Hall and surrounding offices dwindled in favour of the Pink Elephant, as Sebastian had renamed it because he thought it was a rather clever *double entendre*.

It was Nigel Pollock to whom he was most grateful for helping him make his dream possible.

'We should do this sort of thing more often,' Ian said, breathing in the air, rich with the tang of kelp, as he watched the boat owners in the harbour working or enjoying their leisure. 'It's beautiful, isn't it?' They had walked from their hotel on the beach side of the peninsula with its view of Pendennis Castle and the open sea across to where the docks and the quays and the village of Flushing were visible.

They had breakfasted in the overwarm glass-sided extension of the hotel dining-room but Ian had been compensated for this small discomfort by discovering there were scallops on the menu. It was nine thirty, they had the morning to themselves as they were not meeting Mark until twelve. He was at the Falmouth School of Art and last night they had had the dubious pleasure of being introduced to his girlfriend who had joined them, seemingly without invitation, for a seafood meal in a restaurant in Arwenack Street. Afterwards they had said they were going on to a party.

'Strange girl,' Ian remarked, watching an inexperienced sailor capsize his dinghy. Twenty years of marriage had attuned their minds. Moira had been about to make a similar remark. Their son's previous girlfriends had been attractive and intelligent, but always reasonably conventional. This one was the exception. Lara was painfully thin with a mass of hennaed, pre-Raphaelite hair which looked too heavy for such a small body to cope with. The pallor of her skin suggested she only went out at night and her clothes were an assortment of layers in black and purple and

9

badly in need of ironing. By comparison Mark, in clean jeans and a polo shirt, was extremely smart. Moira was pleased to see he radiated health. His skin was lightly tanned, his hair, as blond as his mother's, lightened further by the sun, and there was no hint of tiredness or dullness about the blue eyes. In response to her question as to what he wanted to do in the future he said he still didn't know.

'He's changed,' Ian said as they strolled along Customs House Quay. 'Remember when he was so certain about everything? From the time he started at the comprehensive he was determined to get to an art college, now he hasn't a clue what he wants to do.'

'It's early days. He'll get some guidance later. Besides, it's a time to enjoy life not worry about the future. That's half the point of it, you know, learning to socialise and getting to know yourself.' Moira was recalling her own college days.

'I thought the idea was to get a degree or a qualification.'

'Yes, that too, but it's not the be all and end all. It's a taste of freedom, a break between the discipline of school and the responsibility of being an adult.'

'Discipline of school? You could've fooled me. Last time I was up at the –'

'Don't start on about that again, Ian. You're such a reactionary, times have changed.'

'You're telling me,' he muttered as the skipper of a pleasure boat shouted that trips for the Helford River and the River Fal were available from the Prince of Wales Pier. They decided they just had time for the hour and a half cruise before meeting Mark.

The narrow streets were congested with cars and holiday-makers but they boarded with five minutes to spare. Ian's arms were red when they returned and stood patiently waiting until Mark arrived, fifteen minutes late and with Lara in tow. Moira winked at Ian behind their backs. It was a gesture of commiseration and warning, she might be more forthcoming on a second meeting. But the sullen silence continued.

'It's his choice,' Moira commented on Sunday as they began

the tedious journey home. The car windows were open but it was still sticky.

'I know, but she's so . . . I don't know.'

'Not what you expected. Mark seems happy enough, that's what counts. She's probably quite different when they're alone.'

'She needs to be.'

'I'll drive when we get to Exter.' Moira decided it was time to drop the subject. They were not going to have a break until they were the other side of Plymouth. Recent improvements meant there was dual carriageway down most of the spine of Cornwall but there were still some single-lane roads with no chance of overtaking because of the endless stream of cars and caravans. They had picked one of the busiest weekends to visit Mark.

From Exeter there were motorways as far as Essex where they would have to leave the M25 and join the A12. Some day, Ian thought, he'd like to retire to Cornwall. But for the moment Suffolk was home.

It was late afternoon when they arrived back, the house stuffy and airless because the windows had been shut. They had stopped twice for petrol and coffee but no food because they had overdone breakfast. Ian had taken the Friday off and they had travelled down on Thursday evening but it felt as if they had been away longer than three nights. They would have to eat out as Moira had defrosted both fridge and freezer.

'You've really caught the sun,' she said as she stepped into the shower after Ian. There was a dark V at his neck and a distinct demarcation line where his short-sleeved shirt ended.

They were going to have a Chinese but called into the Crown first. Moira smiled indulgently when Ian picked up his pint of Adnams and studied the clear, amber liquid with an expression akin to reverence before he took the first, welcome sip.

2

'Did you have a good time?'

'Great, thanks.'

'Mark OK?'

'He's fine.' Detective Chief Inspector Ian Roper was not about to discuss his son's love life with Detective Sergeant Barry Swan. He had already put Lara out of his mind. He followed Barry into the general office for the day's briefing which he was not giving himself because he did not know what had happened over the weekend. Initially it appeared nothing much had altered in his absence.

DC Brenda Gibbons explained that on Friday she had been called to a house in Maple Grove regarding a possible missing persons case. She had taken it upon herself to make some preliminary inquiries but as Bruce Selby was a forty-three-year-old single man the Superintendent had advised her not to waste too much time on it. 'He doesn't have a record, sir, and he's not married. Lives with his mother and other family members.'

Adults disappear all the time, often for a variety of perfectly acceptable reasons, sometimes not, as in Selby's case. An all-out effort was only made for the young and the vulnerable. 'What does he do, this Selby?'

'He's a surveyor. No need to work but keeps his hand in. Works from home, apparently, uses his dressing-room off his bedroom as an office. Oh, and he's on the council.'

'Ah, I thought I recognised the name. Go and see the family again. Better safe than sorry.'

12

DC Gibbons, long brown hair gleaming, her small teeth white against her suntanned face, made her way out to the car-park passing WPC Judy Robbins on the way. Sickening, Judy thought, gazing after the slender figure. Some people have all the luck. Judy's hair was also dark, nearly black, but short and she was a stone overweight with the type of pale, opaque skin which burned but never tanned. Her nose was red after an afternoon in the garden. She stomped up the stairs to report to her sergeant wondering why, in that case, she liked Brenda so much. The Chief's back today, she thought, I must find out how Mark's doing. She had babysat on many occasions when he was small.

'This Bruce Selby,' Ian said to Barry as he sifted through the reports and information accumulated during the past three days. 'What do we know about him?'

'Not a lot. Leads a quiet life, shuts himself up in his room a lot and he's never done anything like this before. He went out on Wednesday night and hasn't been seen or heard of since. He didn't make it to the council meeting on Thursday, one of his colleagues rang his home because it was unlike him. He has a reputation for being reliable and punctual. Brenda checked the hospitals and with Traffic. No record of any accident. Oh, and the car's missing.'

'Sounds like he's just bogged off. Had enough of Mummy, maybe. What about clothes?'

'Mrs Selby isn't sure. He isn't a suit man, he favours slacks and a jacket but he has an assortment so she couldn't say if anything had been taken. His passport's in the file along with her own. Brenda said Mrs Selby had her suspicions he might be seeing a woman on the quiet. Married, maybe.'

'Ah.' The word was drawn out as if Barry's last comment explained it all. 'It's still puzzling, though, why a man with no ties and no financial worries should do a bunk. Forty-three, you say?'

'Yes. Unless he's got something to hide, got himself caught up in something illegal and needs to lie low.'

Hundreds of people went missing each year, some simply to start a new life or to shake off the dust of the old, teenagers ran away after family quarrels and men and women ran off with other men and women. Priority was given to minors, the elderly and/or confused and those with a history of psychiatric illness. Bruce Selby fitted none of these categories so it was difficult to know how much manpower and time, if any, to use looking for him.

'It's not as if he's going to lose his job,' Ian said thoughtfully, 'not if he's self-employed and got a private income anyway. We'll wait and see if DC Gibbons comes back with anything.' He took out a file which he was preparing for the DPP's office, although he knew in advance the case would be thrown out. All the evidence was circumstantial and they had been unable to get a confession. Still, you never knew.

DS Swan was on his way to interview a witness who claimed to have seen something concerning a break-in at the back of one of the shops in the High Street, but as no accommodation overlooked the unloading area the only way this was possible was for him to have been there sometime around 2 a.m. Not impossible, though. He might have pulled in for a bit of a fumble with his girlfriend.

Ian put the file in his out-tray and stared at the other papers accumulated on his desk. There was a long, complicated memo about the reorganisation of night duties, another memo stating that alterations were about to begin in the canteen but it would still be partially functioning, although why these were necessary when the purpose-built station house had only been inhabited for five years was beyond him. No doubt it was something to do with the budget. A liaison meeting with neighbourhood watch residents was imminent, the uniformed lot would oblige there, the rest was a waste of paper.

He rang his secretary and asked her to fetch some coffee. 'Black, no sugar,' he said. He had overdone the food at the weekend, a few days' abstention was called for.

His secretary, Gina, found him in a familiar pose, his chair tilted back, his hands clasped behind his head and a blank expression on his face, which meant he was thinking. He always appeared too large for normal office furniture; his six-foot, four-inch frame

14

was broad and solid with a tendency to put on weight if he wasn't careful. Although he was not conventionally good-looking, most people liked his lived-in face and he was proud of his thick hair even if it was greying slightly at the temples.

'Ah, Gina, thanks.' He registered her presence.

'Need me for anything? Only I'm still catching up on last week's correspondence.'

'Not at the moment. Hold on, you could read this and summarise it for me. One page'll do.'

She tutted as she took the sheaf of paper, wondering why anyone bothered to write such long memos when no one ever bothered to read them. She went back to her office leaving Ian in the same position as when she first came in.

If I were Selby, he thought, comfortably off, no wife, no apparent worries, why would I want to disappear without leaving word with anyone? I wouldn't. Not unless it was to be permanent for some reason. It was not his case but it was intriguing. Successful disappearances fascinated him and he wondered how often it had been achieved. Of course, there was a more sinister aspect. Supposing Selby had not chosen to go missing? The family were wealthy enough to pay a substantial ransom, or perhaps he was lying dead somewhere, a heart attack, say, the body not yet discovered.

There could, of course, be a yet more sinister reason. Lord Lucan had everything going for him yet he had found it necessary to disappear, one way or another. The thought was depressing; Ian did not want something similar hanging over his head. It might, therefore, be an idea to go through any outstanding crimes and not necessarily just in his own area.

The chair tilted forward with a jolt causing Ian to knock his knee on the edge of the desk. Selby. The name rang a bell. His memory was not far off infallible when it came to policing; domestic events were another matter. Somehow he was certain it was not just because he had subconsciously taken in the fact that the man was on the local council.

He picked up the internal phone and requested any information on file concerning the Selbys to be dug up immediately. 'Go back as far as you can,' he instructed. 'In fact, start around 1960.' A not uncommon feeling of smugness lasted until the telephone rang some time later.

'There's nothing, sir,' the disembodied voice informed him. 'We went further back than that but the name doesn't crop up at all.'

'Thank you.' For nothing, he added silently. Then why was he sure there was something? It was more than wishful thinking.

He had been a young officer, Ian was sure of that, when the name had cropped up. Whatever the circumstances it was obvious no charges had been brought. Perhaps if he took a run out to the address something would jolt his memory. Later, maybe, on his way home. For now there was what appeared to be half a rain forest waiting to be dealt with in the in-tray.

For another forty-five minutes he conscientiously made his eyes slide over the various sheets of paper whilst he kidded himself he was reading but his thoughts kept reverting to the name Selby.

'Damn it.' He balled the memo concerning the canteen and chucked it in the direction of the waste-paper basket.

'It's deliberate, why won't anyone believe me?'

Sergeant Whitelaw smiled indulgently at the diminutive, elderly lady whose head barely came above the level of the counter in the reception area. This was not the first time she had been in and he suspected her visits might be due to loneliness or even the onset of paranoia which sometimes strikes with old age. She lived alone in a two-up, two-down property in Railway Terrace, once a busy area which had become run down and seedy, shops boarded up waiting for the inevitable demolition which had drastically altered that end of Rickenham. Sergeant Whitelaw barely remembered what had once stood in certain areas. Beeching had seen to it that the station was no more than a branch line and the rusted, weed-covered metal of disused tracks was the only evidence there had once been a thriving goods yard. However, some of the properties which had been bought up by people with foresight had been done up and were fast becoming desirable residences. A bit like Docklands in London, he thought as he listened to the complainant.

'All right, Mrs Mostyn, how about if I send someone round to have a word with you, see if there's anything we can think of to help stop it happening again.'

Satisfied that something was going to be done she hobbled off towards the revolving doors in her summer blouse and skirt.

It was true she had suffered more than her share of vandalism but it was rife in that part of the town. Her windows had been smashed four times in as many weeks and she was worried about the insurance. Graffiti had been scrawled on the brick wall at the back and her gate broken. She had been to stay with her daughter for a few days and returned to find her dustbin over-turned, rubbish scattered all over the yard and more daubs on the house itself. Impossible to trace the culprit because it might have been done as long as six days ago.

Sergeant Whitelaw made a note to see if the community constable could have a word. At least she would feel there was someone on her side.

DC Brenda Gibbons drove across town to Maple Grove wishing she was still on the beach at Aldeburgh, where she had spent the weekend with a friend. Sunlight dancing off wing mirrors and the bodywork of cars was dazzling. She parked in the wide road, which was free from restrictions. It was a good address to pos-sess. Doc Harris, GP and one of their police surgeons, lived down there somewhere, but in one of the smaller houses further on.

Mrs Selby had said she would be at home all day on Monday if anyone wished to contact her, so no appointment was necessary. It was eleven fifteen when Brenda knocked on the door. Elizabeth Selby answered it, having told the woman who came in to do the housework that she would get it herself. The woman was a gossip, there was no need to fuel the fire.

She was dressed in a cream linen suit and tan low-heeled court shoes although her legs were bare. The short sleeves of the jacket revealed golden skin but it was lacking elasticity and slightly freckled. Other than that she displayed no signs of any of the infirmities which can afflict the over-sixties.

'There's still no news,' she said, recognising Brenda and directing her to the back of the house. The strain was beginning to show. There were dark circles beneath her eyes which were dulled with lack of sleep.

Outside on the terrace was some garden furniture; a paperback, open, face down, lay on the table, the cover curling in the sun as if it had not been picked up for some time. 'Please, sit down. Would you like a drink of something?'

'I'd love a cup of tea.' Brenda sat beneath the blue and white striped sunshade wondering why anyone would wish to escape from the beautiful house and grounds. It was a ridiculous thought springing from her own recently acquired security and the warmth of the morning. Material possessions were simply that and had no sway over emotions.

Elizabeth Selby took more time than was necessary to prepare the tray of tea. Brenda guessed she needed a few minutes to gather her thoughts, perhaps she had been expecting her to have come with good news.

'I'm not some over-protective mother making a fuss,' she said as she poured the tea. 'Bruce is in his forties, he's a free agent, but this is the first time he has not let one of us know where he is. It's just so . . . so unlike him.'

'You said he does stay away sometimes?'

'Yes, occasionally for one night, but he always says because whoever is last in is responsible for locking up and switching on the burglar alarm. He has a boat, he goes there sometimes.'

'You think that's what he's done? Taken a few days away from it all?'

'No. Not without telling me.'

Brenda noted down the details of the moorings on the Norfolk Broads. 'But you think he might be seeing a girlfriend?'

Elizabeth smiled wryly. 'Girlfriend hardly seems appropriate for someone of Bruce's age, but yes, he had taken to showering again in the evening if he was going out. But I've no idea who it might be, he never brings anyone home.'

'Mrs Selby, I'd like you to make a list of everyone your son knows or might know.' Brenda swallowed the last of the scented China tea. 'I realise there'll be some acquaintances you're not aware of, but we'll take it from there.'

'You're taking this seriously, aren't you?' It made her more worried.

'We take all unexplained disappearances seriously.' Not strictly true, but the woman was in need of reassurance. From the little she knew of Bruce Selby he did not seem the type to cause undue anxiety. On her first visit his brother, Maurice, and his wife had shown equal concern. It was they who had persuaded Elizabeth to ring the police.

Elizabeth forced herself into the role of hostess. 'I expect there's a simple explanation, an accident, maybe, and Bruce has amnesia. Would you like more tea?'

'No, thanks.' Brenda did not disillusion her. She had already stated that Bruce would have had plenty of identification on him. 'Would you object if I took a look at his room?'

'Whatever for? Forgive me, that was rude. You surprised me. Of course you can.'

She followed Mrs Selby up the stairs and was shown the relevant door. 'I'd prefer you to stay,' Brenda said.

It was a decent-sized bedroom with a double bed, a dressing-table and a small desk and chair. The wardrobes were built in across one wall and contained slacks and jackets, some of which were in dry cleaner's polythene wrapping. Below were shoes on a rack, and shirts and underwear were neatly folded on open shelves.

'Bruce always saw to his own clothes and the woman who comes in to clean washes and irons his shirts. I still can't say if there's anything missing.'

One of the dressing-table drawers held sweaters, the others were full of stationery and old invoices which had been paid.

There was nothing on the bedside table apart from a lamp, an alarm clock and a book on waterways.

The desk contained nothing but pens, headed notepaper and envelopes and a few pieces of personal correspondence; the walk-in dressing-room, Bruce's office, told the same story. The desk there held papers and a copy of a recent communication stapled to his report on a house he had surveyed. The neatly set out typing was courtesy of the small word processor on the desk. There was, Brenda decided, not a single item in the room which suggested the man's character apart from the book on canals.

The room itself hinted at Mrs Selby's choice of furnishings, the theme floral without being overtly feminine. Two incongruous, heavily framed oil paintings may have been selected by Bruce but they hung at a disadvantage against the sprigged flower background. During the hour of her visit DC Gibbons realised she had gleaned nothing new.

'I'll let you have that list tomorrow,' Mrs Selby said as she showed her out.

'Thanks.' She felt sorry for the woman. No matter how old your children, they still remained a worry.

Suicide crossed her mind as she turned the car around. Selby's room was devoid of personality: perhaps the man himself had become so and found a way out. No. Suddenly she realised how very neat the room was, everything in its place, except for the jacket hung over the back of the chair. Bruce Selby had intended returning.

PC Mallet was not a man easily ruffled. Years of being a figure of fun had taught him it was no good getting wound up, life was too short to allow the gibes to hurt. It had surprised his parents when he had applied to join the police because the helmet would emphasise his exceptional height. He was two inches taller than DCI Roper; the apex of his helmet, when worn, was over seven feet from the ground. Added to this was a reedy body which was fitter than it appeared but gave him cause to wish they still had the authority to clip kids around the ear. How many more times would one ask if it was cold up there? Yet these points had their advantages. As a community policeman everyone soon got to know him. Mr Gilbert, a pensioner, always waited to see him pass and would have a chat or ask him to have a look at his latest water-colour. Young mothers were grateful for his assistance in handling prams up steps and local shopkeepers knew he kept an eye on their premises or warned them if there had been a spate of burglaries. He was approachable, which was exactly what he was there for.

He knew Violet Mostyn slightly, she would bob her head at him when he passed and he would touch his helmet in the old-fashioned way which, he knew, pleased her. He knew about her broken windows and the graffiti but these incidents had taken place at night when he was not on duty and she had told him she preferred to report them at the station.

Sergeant Whitelaw had asked him to have a word. He wasted no time in doing so. There was no need to knock, Mrs Mostyn was on the pavement, balanced on a kitchen stool, cleaning her downstairs window. 'It'll be a waste of time,' she said. 'They'll be smashed again presently.'

'That's what I've come to talk to you about.'

'They said they'd send someone. I thought it would be a detective. I really don't see what you can do about it apart from having a man stand guard, back and front, twenty-four hours a day. And you'll never arrest the culprit because no one believes me.'

'Well, who do you think is responsible?'

'I told them down at the station, whoever it is is someone who wants me out of here.'

'Who'd want you out, Mrs Mostyn?' Bill Whitelaw might be right; a touch of paranoia?

'Somebody does, I'm sure of it. Why don't they do it next door?'

'Next door is empty.'

'There you are. Precisely. The little tearaways that live round here haven't touched the place, the upstairs windows are all intact.' The lower ones were boarded up.

PC Mallet saw her point. It might be that a couple of young-sters took delight in frightening the old lady but he knew most of them in the district and the ones he had spoken to had denied it. He gave her some advice on security at which she sniffed in disgust and asked if it wouldn't be better if the streets were properly policed at night. 'A patrol car down here now and again might be enough to deter the little buggers,' she said.

PC Mallet said he would pass her thoughts on. He had ex-pected to be offered a cup of tea, he was thirsty, but no such offer was forthcoming. He would have to make do with Mr Gilbert's weak brew about which he did not complain because he was aware the elderly man used the tea-bags more than once because his financial position dictated this necessary economy.

Ian had driven slowly down Maple Grove, half tempted to call in for a quick snifter with the Doc, whose car was parked in his drive. But Moira was expecting him. The Selby house was set back from the road and protected by a high hedge. Yes, he thought, he had definitely been to the house before, but not recently. The obvious explanation was that there had been an attempted break-in, it was the sort of place which would tempt thieves by virtue of its size and the fact that the trees and shrubs provided plenty of protection from prying eyes. That would explain why there was no record of the event. Unsuccessful intruders who had taken nothing and had not been caught, that was the answer. So why did he think it wasn't? 'Goddammit,' he swore as he made his way home. It was nothing to do with him anyway and DC Gibbons was more than capable of dealing with it.

The following day DC Gibbons came to his office to ask what, if anything, she should do next. It was Tuesday, almost time to pack up and go home, and there had still been no more news concerning Bruce Selby's whereabouts. Ian shook his head. 'I don't know. I think we should keep looking, though.'

More puzzling was that there was no possible link between Selby and any undetected crimes, at least not serious ones, not in Rickenham Green nor anywhere else, and his movements had been accounted for by his family, his clients and his council colleagues until the time of his disappearance.

'I've got to know,' Ian decided. 'I think I'll go and see the family myself.'

'You'll put Brenda's nose out of joint,' DS Swan told him.

'Maybe, but we're not here to pander to each other's egos.'

'Without the Super's approval?' Superintendent Thorne believed that if you were entrusted to a job, you got on with it without interference from higher up.

'I do not need Mike Thorne's approval for my actions, Barry.'

'Touchy, aren't we? It's just that this isn't some inadequate, or some person at risk.'

'No, but we're going to look bloody fools if his body turns up in a ditch and we've done bugger all to find him.'

'Brenda's been trying. But point taken. Fancy a pint?'

'When don't I? How about the Feathers, we can sit in the garden.'

Barry was surprised, Ian preferred the Crown because it sold Adnams bitter.

'Lucy out tonight?'

'My wife has informed me that she has an appointment after work and she won't be home until seven thirty.'

'Secrets already?' Barry and Lucy had been married just over a year. Previously there had been an endless string of females, then he met Lucy when he transferred his account to the bank in which she worked because he was fed up with the poor service he was getting elsewhere. It was one of life's oddities that he had not met her before because Lucy had gone to school with WPC Judy Robbins and they had remained friends ever since. Judy was grateful to her friend for ridding Barry of his somewhat arrogant manner.

Nigel Pollock was not a man to have qualms about being seen in the Pink Elephant because he had no doubts concerning his own sexuality. His wife, Anne-Marie, had none either; she found him a little too demanding but it was a small price to pay for the lifestyle he provided. She did, however, draw the line at sending the boys away to school because she would have missed them. Nigel had money when she met him and had made a success of his business. If his deals weren't always strictly straight, it was no concern of hers and a subject they did not discuss.

Nigel's relationship with Sebastian Roberts was business. Sebastian had come to him by chance, recommended by word of mouth. Pollock's company had a good name for quality work and Nigel had done the boy a favour. The favour had been returned although Sebastian Roberts was not aware of it.

'Evening.' Nigel stood at the bar.

'Hi. Usual?' Sebastian pushed a cut glass tumbler under the optic, waited for it to refill then repeated the action. 'On the house,' he said, placing it on the bar.

'Cheers. Chaz around?'

'No.' Sebastian frowned. 'I haven't seen him for a while, come to think of it.' In his trade one day ran into the next.

'Not been in at all?'

'He's got boyfriend trouble, I believe, he was quite upset last time I saw him.'

'No matter. Is Leon around?'

'He said he'll be in about eight. He's getting me some cheap hanging baskets for the front.'

'It'll look nice,' Nigel told him, but his mind was elsewhere.

'Go on, why not?'

'Why? is more to the point.'

'Because I'm curious, Ian.'

He had already resigned himself to the fact that he would have to take Moira to the Pink Elephant for a drink because if he didn't she would ring her friend Deirdre and he'd have to spend the evening on his own. What the fascination was in a pub full of queers was beyond him. Gays, he reminded himself, having

24

been brought up in another age with different terminology and attitudes. Despite which he still thought it was an inapt description. The ones he had met had been depressed, on drugs, or had a chip on their shoulder. But then, he reasoned, everyone who crossed his path professionally was either a victim, a suspect or in some sort of trouble. He should know better than to discriminate. Should, and did, but although he would never voice his opinions some of his father's prejudices had rubbed off. Moira, on the other hand, really didn't seem to give a damn.

They strolled down Belmont Terrace in the warm evening air. At the T-junction they turned left into a wider, tree-lined street. Pigeons bathed in the dust where the grass verge was wearing thin and there was an uncanny stillness because the traffic was light. People were eating their meals or watching television or enjoying their gardens. In the small playing field a group of children ran and shouted, their voices reverberating as they castigated a border collie who kept chasing their ball. In another five minutes they were in Buckton Road.

'It's very smart for the area,' Moira commented when they had taken their drinks to a table.

Ian grinned at her, relieved to find it was a great improvement on what had been the Prince William. 'And you're a very smart piece for an ageing DCI.' She was wearing ecru slacks and a loose, cream blouse which suited her slender figure. Her pale hair was tied back and the flat sandals meant she only came up to his shoulder. He hoped, as had happened once or twice, no one mistook her for his daughter. He could never bring himself to forget the fifteen-year discrepancy in their ages and when he was tired or irritable that gap might have been double. It was no longer a mystery why Moira had chosen him, it was why she stayed that puzzled him.

'It's not what I expected,' Ian admitted, although exactly what that was he would have been hard pushed to say. It was certainly tastefully furnished and decorated without being over the top, and the Adnams was in perfect condition, but he had to admit he was not entirely comfortable. As the Prince William it had been the haunt of police informers and minor criminals. Sebastian Roberts was having none of that and they had decamped to the Black Horse in Saxborough Road. DS Markham, Ian thought, used to frequent the place to get his information.

To humour Moira they stayed for a second drink. There were several customers but no one took any notice when he went up to the bar to buy it. A big, bull-necked man smiled and Ian returned it, there was nothing limp-wristed about him.

'We'll have to go, I've left the meal in the oven.' Heat was still rising from the pavements as they walked home and shrubs and trees were wilting, covered in their urban layer of diesel and dust. Rain was badly needed, the floods of the previous winter were no more than a memory.

They ate in the garden despite the midges. 'If he's lucky, Mark'll get the last of the runner beans,' Moira said, nodding towards the few remaining red flowers around the cane wigwam. His summer job was coming to an end and he was going to spend the last two weeks of the vacation at home. He was supplementing his grant, he had told them, but Moira suspected it had more to do with Lara remaining in Falmouth.

They watched the nine o'clock news and the weather and waited for the local news. 'Something must've happened,' Ian said, leaning forward eagerly. 'The Super's really taking it seriously.' There had been a brief request for Bruce Selby to make his whereabouts known to his family or at any police station.

As Ian spoke the telephone rang.

3

The fact that the temperature that evening was more usually associated with European holidays had not concerned Sandra and James Wright as they ambled along beside the bank of the river where, for once, it was dry underfoot. To their right only a thin stream trickled over the stones and on the other bank was open meadow, the grass long and interwoven with wild flowers. A few red poppy petals were clinging to their calyxes, the first casualties of the beginning of the end of summer.

They had taken the path under the stone road bridge, covered the small meadow on their bank and were now heading towards a wooded area. None of these things registered because Sandra and James Wright were trying to decide if their marriage was worth saving. At least, Sandra was. Now the children had left home she felt that her life had come to an impasse, that she and her husband seemed to have very little in common. 'It's the indifference,' she said.

'Yours or mine? I don't think I treat you indifferently. I try to make you happy. I don't want it to end, Sandra.'

'I don't think you've really thought about it, you're just saying that because it's the easy option.'

'And you're saying it to make it easier for you to leave.'

'I just don't know any more.' She walked on, a little faster, leaving a space of a few yards between them because she felt trapped by his persistence and the dawning knowledge that he did still love her.

'Sandra, wait. We've too much to lose. I'll do anything you want.'

'I know that.' She turned away. 'But the thing is . . . Oh, Jesus. Oh, my God. James, look.' But before he had a chance to see what she meant Sandra had fallen on her knees and was vomiting into the undergrowth.

DC Brenda Gibbons was one of the first to be informed and therefore one of the first at the scene. It was, after all, her case. No wonder Bruce Selby had not called home. She had been half expecting, half dreading this because the more time that passed, the more certain she was becoming that the Bruce Selbys of this world do not simply take a hike. The rest of the troops had already been marshalled.

'He's the right age and build, sir,' she said when DCI Roper arrived. 'But other than that . . .' She waved a dismissive hand. The victim lay face down and the weather and the wildlife had left their mark.

'We'll wait for the lights.' Ian moved some distance away and lit a cigarette. Plodding along under the bridge he saw the familiar rotund shape of Doc Harris. The sky was a purple grey as dusk descended. Under the trees in full leaf and amongst the undergrowth it was impossible to work without lighting.

'Get someone to drive them home,' he instructed the uniformed PC who was comforting the Wrights. 'They can make their statements in the morning.' There was no urgency, they had not stumbled on a newly executed crime. They had both gone to the telephone box at the top of the High Street and been asked to wait so they could show the police where the body was.

A quarter moon and pink streaks appeared in the darkening sky and then the sudden glare of the arc lights, set up to illuminate the grotesqueness of death.

'I can't be certain,' Brenda said without a sign of squeamishness when the photographers, Doc Harris and the Home Office pathologist had done their stuff and the body was turned over, 'but his own mother wouldn't recognise him now.' She wished she hadn't said it, someone from the Selby family would be asked to do just that.

It was almost 3 a.m. before Ian returned home, leaving Forensics, in the capable hands of their leader, John Cotton, to finish off their business. A wider search of the area would have to be left until the morning which meant some poor sod had to stand guard all night making sure nobody entered the area surrounded by tape. In weather like this it was not unlikely that a courting couple might take advantage of the privacy of the woods. To the right was running water, albeit running slowly, but any evidence in that direction would have been washed away. Ian was driven home, glad to be away from the stench of decomposition and the earthy smell of vegetation.

He allowed himself four hours' sleep, which was enough to get by on for a limited period.

'White male, somewhere between thirty and fifty,' Ian said in response to Barry's question.

'You were right.'

'About what?'

'Him turning up in a ditch. Just as well Brenda went back, it won't look so bad for us. Have the family been informed?'

'Brenda volunteered to see them, she said she had built up a rapport with Mrs Selby.' Later one of them would have to come in to make a formal identification. Meanwhile the body had been removed to the hospital mortuary to await the post-mortem and all units had been alerted to find Selby's car in which the 'murderer' may have been a passenger.

'Suspicious death?'

'Without question. Even if he died from natural causes the body had been moved. Dragged quite a few yards by the look of it.' Luckily there had been no rain and the broken twigs and flattened area were undisturbed. 'But neither the Doc nor the pathologist was able to give the cause of death. There's a head wound, though.'

Barry did not like to inquire as to the state of the body. He'd find out soon enough at the dreaded PM.

The incident room was set up in the station. There were no houses in the vicinity of the river and drivers of cars passing over the narrow, humped stone bridge would not, even if they had been looking, have been able to see anything over its walls. Everything could be dealt with more efficiently from base.

Ian hoped he had not disturbed Moira but she had only muttered and turned over when he finally climbed into bed and he had left just as she was waking up. She had changed jobs and did not need to leave the house until eight forty as she was now the personal assistant to the owner of a small chain of garages which sold top of the range models. It also meant she got a discount on petrol. He was rather proud of her.

John Cotton's team had returned to the scene after a break of a couple of hours, time in which, Ian knew, John would have drunk several pints of milky coffee and emptied a packet of Marlboro cigarettes. Because dawn was around five it had not been worth them going home and they needed to search before more people tramped all over the area. It was surprising, and fortunate, kids hadn't come across the body because school holidays were still in progress.

It was always like this, Ian's mind spinning and racing, trying to make some sense out of it before he had the facts.

At ten thirty, starting to feel gritty-eyed, but satisfied that everyone knew their role and was sticking to it, he went down to the canteen for coffee and toast, able, he felt, to face food now. Policeman or not, last night's findings had not done his stomach any good.

The Wrights had come in early, presumably because they were unable to sleep, and made individual statements but they were not under any suspicion.

DS Markham was ahead of him in the short queue. Ian followed him to a table, his stomach rumbling after fourteen hours without food.

'Only one of my informers has even heard of him,' Markham

said. He had been asked to make a few subtle inquiries about Selby. 'And that's only because he reads the *Herald* from cover to cover and knew he was a local councillor.'

Ian dipped his spoon in the sugar bowl but restricted himself to the once. Markham, with his expressionless pale blue eyes and his cropped hair, exuded menace. No one had been able to work out if this was a persona he had adopted, the way he really was or an unfortunate trick of nature disguising the real man. Unorthodox in his approach he might be, difficult to work with he certainly was, but no one could deny his record of arrests was excellent; it was therefore best not to question his methods too deeply.

The coffee was tepid, the dregs of one of the two filter jugs. Ian took it back and asked for a replacement which was given to him without comment from the sullen girl who worked when Betty wasn't on duty.

'Is it him? Selby?' Markham asked when Ian returned.

'It's got to be, hasn't it?' The detectives working through the night had checked their missing persons files, no one else fitted the rough description closely enough. Now all they had to do was find the killer. No, not necessarily the killer, but whoever had moved the body.

Or so he thought.

'It isn't him, sir. It isn't Bruce Selby.'

'What?'

'His mother confirmed it this morning. Apart from the fact he doesn't own a leather jacket or a wrist-watch like the one we showed her, she says her son has an appendicectomy scar and a large mole on his right calf. Also, Bruce Selby is thicker set and his torso less hairy.'

'But . . .'

'She wasn't in any doubt, sir, it wasn't wishful thinking.'

There were no operation scars or large moles on the body. There were a lot of other marks, though. The leather jacket had protected the torso, likewise the shoes, the feet. Mrs Selby had not been subjected to seeing the state of the head.

The maggots in the eye sockets had been sent for entomology tests. It was likely to be the only way a reasonably accurate date of death could be predicted. Likewise, a specialist odontologist would now have to be called in if they were to have any chance of identifying the victim. But tests took time. Had they been able to put a name to the man, they would have had a base from which to work, tracing his last steps. Not, Ian reminded himself, that they had got very far with Bruce Selby.

The post-mortem would have to go ahead without an official identification. In this case continuity of evidence would have to suffice and the procedure had been followed to the letter, a PC travelling in the van which removed the body to the mortuary.

If Selby isn't the victim, Ian thought, then could he possibly be the murderer?

Sergeant Whitelaw, on another early shift but not minding as he liked to watch the racing on the television in the afternoons, watched Mrs Mostyn struggle through the revolving doors. 'Hello,' he said, 'back to see us again?'

'I don't know what you're grinning for. That tall chap, PC Mallet they call him, he came round like you said – fat lot of good he did.'

'More problems?'

'The insurance people.' She fumbled in her handbag and withdrew a piece of paper. 'A case number, that's what I need. Proof that I reported the vandalism or some such thing. An excuse to get out of paying if you ask me.'

'No problem.' Bill Whitelaw did not point out that he had issued one on her previous visit. She was elderly and frail and probably a bit forgetful. He wrote out the details and handed them to her. Her eyes were moist but she did not cry.

'It's my home,' she said, 'I've lived there almost fifty years, ever since I got married. I don't want to leave, I want to die there, not be shoved in some home.'

Bill Whitelaw lifted the flap of the counter and led her to a seat, his arm across her shoulder. 'Sit down for a minute, love. I'll get some tea sent up.'

'Tea won't help.' But she took the proffered chair and composed herself, not wishing him to think her an old fool.

Was there some sort of vendetta in progress? he wondered. No one else from Railway Terrace had been having the same problems.

Sebastian Roberts was pleased his advert in the *Rickenham Herald* had paid off. There was hardly a spare seat by nine thirty on Wednesday evening. He was introducing live music twice a week and the local band he had hired was good and had pulled in some new faces. Two men seated near the open door were strangers and far from inconspicuous. 'A bit OTT, don't you think?' he said to the barmaid as they both pulled pints of bitter. One wore jeans and a T-shirt, a stud in his ear and a small ring through his nose, and was darkly handsome, the other was dressed in salmon pink jeans stretched tautly against his skin.

Aware that he was being watched, the dark man approached the bar. 'Has Chaz Carlos been in tonight? Only we're friends of his from way back and we were told he drinks here.'

'Haven't seen him for a while.' Sebastian frowned. Only recently had he mentioned his absence to Nigel Pollock. Perhaps he was doing his drinking elsewhere. 'You can leave a message if you like, I'll make sure he gets it.'

'Thanks. Got a piece of paper?'

The man wrote down his name and a telephone number. 'That's where we're staying, but we're only there until Saturday. I like the music,' he added. 'We'll call in again.'

Sebastian put the note behind an optic along with several other messages. He did not mind acting as a free post office, it meant customers returned to pick up messages.

He turned to check his appearance in the mirror-backed shelves, hating to appear anything other than immaculate. Like most of the clientele he was in jeans but his had a sharp crease down the centre leg and his shirt was crisp striped cotton. His hair was razor cut at the sides and gelled on top. When he turned around he saw Leon Dawson had just come in. Leon knew Chaz better than anyone, he might know where he was.

'No, haven't seen him since sometime last week. Why?'

'I just wondered. No one else's seen him either and there's two people over there asking for him.'

Leon turned around and followed the direction of Sebastian's eyes. 'I've never seen them before, they're not local.' His tone conveyed unconcealed dislike. He hated that sort, so obviously camp, the type that gave them all a bad name and caused them to be the butt of jokes. 'Still, I can't say I'm surprised at Chaz.'

The band was taking a break and the players came to the bar for a drink. Sebastian refused their money and asked if they would be prepared to return on a monthly basis. 'I don't want the same thing every week,' he explained. 'The customers'll get bored. Can you do it?' The four men conferred then agreed.

Sebastian managed to get everyone out within the stipulated drinking-up time: he was not going to fall into the trap of serving after hours, not for anyone, he needed to be sure his licence would be renewed. Even so it was almost one before he had finished cleaning up and putting the chairs and tables back in their usual places. Soon he would employ a daily cleaner but for the moment he was using any spare resources on getting the business going.

There was no television in the bar and he was too tired to listen to the news on the bedside radio. With only a sheet covering him Sebastian enjoyed several minutes of knowing sleep would come easily. He had worked hard and the business was starting to make money. It was a satisfying feeling. He gave little thought to Chaz, who was probably just keeping his head down after the break-up of a long-standing relationship.

34

*

Ian rang the bell of the Selby household and was admitted by a woman who sighed as if she had seen enough of the local constabulary. He knew immediately that he had been inside that house before. He was shown into the large lounge and asked to wait. It was not long before Elizabeth Selby made an appearance. Ian did not recognise her.

'I'm so glad they've got someone more senior on to it,' were her words of greeting once Ian had introduced himself. He let the comment ride.

'DC Gibbons has been working very hard on finding your son, as have other officers who are involved. However, I just wanted to clear up a couple of points.'

'Oh?' Mrs Selby did not look as pleased as she sounded at having a chief inspector involved.

'Mm. I was here once before, you may remember. It was a long time ago, but . . .'

'I doubt that. We are not in the practice of having dealings with the police.'

'No offence meant. Our work is not entirely devoted to crime, sometimes we're the bearers of good news.' Ian was not sure how to continue. Mrs Selby had not denied a previous visit but if he asked outright what it was about, after having admitted he was one of the officers involved, it would make him look as foolish as he felt. 'I expect you miss your husband at times like this.' It was a safe enough remark, Mr Selby had been dead long enough for it not to be upsetting.

'I don't like your attitude, Chief Inspector. You've already mentioned a previous visit then you compound it by saying "at times like this" as if we're one of your problem families.'

'That was not my intention.' It hadn't been, so why, then, was the woman making such a meal of it? There was more to this than the disappearance of her son. Certain that the damage was done and that he would not elicit any further information, Ian decided to cut his losses. The feminine approach was required here, the matriarch apparently resented male interference. It was strange, he thought, as he was shown to the door, how he had instantly gained that impression.

'I'm sorry to have disturbed you.' Ian smiled with what he hoped passed for charm then altered the smile to a puzzled frown. 'Your husband,' he said. 'Old age must be catching up with me, I can't recall his first name.'

'Theobold. Theo to his family.'

'Ah, yes, of course,' but before he could ask the next question the door was closed firmly in his face.

That was all it had needed. The name Theo brought it all back. He would pass on what he knew and see if Brenda Gibbons could make anything of it. The records office was right, Theo Selby had not been charged with anything and, if he recalled correctly, there had been little more than rumour to go on and the hysterical statement of a nine-year-old boy who had been unable to describe the man. Was the Selby clan not quite as squeaky clean as they liked to portray themselves?

DC Brenda Gibbons took note of what the Chief had said but was not sure how to incorporate this information into her inquiries. One thing was certain, she was not satisfied. They had a body and they had a missing person but what she had was a feeling that the Selbys were being economical with the truth. She picked up the list of Bruce's acquaintances with which Mrs Selby had supplied her and began going through the statements they had provided. The reaction was the same in each case: disbelief or shock. Bruce's fellow councillors were equally puzzled. 'We were surprised he didn't turn up, but done a bunk? Never.' And another: 'To be absolutely honest, we always found him to be a little staid and stodgy.' And yet another had said, 'He always likes things just so. I wouldn't want you to repeat it, but he's a bit of an old woman at times. Sorry,' he added, seeing the slightly mocking smile, 'no offence meant.'

Further inquiries showed that Bruce's boat had not left its

moorings for several weeks. She went back to the Selby household convinced she had not been told the whole story.

For the first time, Maurice Selby saw that his mother was no longer young. The lines in her face had deepened almost overnight. The publishing firm for which he worked was happy for him to take a few days off to be with her. His own feelings regarding his brother were a mixture of puzzlement and anger but he did not doubt he was safe. Bruce lived by the book, impossible to imagine him in some sort of trouble. His mother was resting when Brenda Gibbons rang the bell. In an olive pinafore over a white, sleeveless vest, her feet in leather sandals and her coppery brown hair tied back because of the breeze, DC Gibbons appealed to his baser instincts, a fleeting mental adultery, no more than that because few women were more beautiful than his own wife and he valued her love too much to jeopardise it.

'Come in,' he said. 'Mother's lying down, do you need to speak to her?'

'Not really.'

'Come through to the lounge. My wife's at home too. None of us can understand it,' he added as he held the door open. 'Even the children are unsettled. Uncle Bruce is always around.'

Brenda smiled at Norma Selby who stood up when she entered the room. 'Obviously you haven't had any news. Look, is there anything which has occurred to either of you to suggest where he might be?'

Their blank expressions gave her the answer. Norma sat down again. 'I'm beginning to think Elizabeth would've been happier if the body they found was Bruce. It's the uncertainty, you see, it's making her ill.'

'Mrs Selby, how well do you know your brother-in-law?'

'Very. We live in the same house, after all.'

'Is there anything about him you find odd?' A picture was slowly building up. Middle-aged man, single, living at home

37

with the family, pernickety, fastidious even, solitary interests, apart from his position on the council.

'Odd? Not really. I think he would have liked to marry. There have been women, only one or two, but not for long.' She paused. Maurice was staring at her. 'He confided in me, one night after your mother's birthday party. He said he thought there must be something wrong with him because no matter how hard he tried, he seemed to put women off. I think that was the problem, he tried too hard. Flowers, chocolates, always taking their feelings into consideration, worrying about their welfare to the point of over-protection. Ironic, isn't it.' She smiled wryly at Brenda. 'Most females think that's what they want, but it isn't. They want to be treated as fellow human beings, not put on a pedestal.'

Brenda nodded her agreement. 'That's what he confided to you?'

'Well, there was something else. He admitted he had a short-lived affair with a married woman.'

'Norma!'

'I'm sorry, Maurice, but that's what he said. Whether it's true or not is a different matter. Perhaps he was just boasting.' But they both knew Bruce was modest.

Brenda watched the interaction between this middle generation of the Selby family and thought what an incongruous pair they made. Maurice, plump and balding and an old-worldly gentleman, his wife with green eyes and wavy red hair falling to her shoulders and the figure of an Italian film star whose name she could not recall, yet their contentment was apparent.

Norma chewed a thumbnail. 'No, Bruce wasn't odd, just quiet. And like I said, he always tried *too* hard. It's usually the bastards women fall for.'

Brenda laughed. How true. She knew better than most. But she was over it now. 'How long ago was it he told you this?'

'In May. But it happened a long time ago. I think his conscience got the better of him and he needed to get it off his chest. He said he was so relieved the husband never found out. I can imagine how discreet he would have been. Good heavens, you don't think he did find out and has done something awful to Bruce?'

It was a possibility. Murders had been committed for less. Except, as far as they knew, Bruce was still alive.

Norma lit a cigarette, first offering the packet to Brenda, who declined. 'I limit myself to five a day', she said, 'but I need one now.'

'Mrs Selby, who was this woman?'

Norma flushed, then decided to answer the question. 'Patti Evans. Her husband is a cripple. He was involved in some sort of accident and lost the use of his legs. The compensation bought them a specifically designed bungalow and an adequate income. I believe they still live in Rickenham.'

'You seem to know a lot of the details.'

'Yes. I have never mentioned this to anyone before. Bruce seemed to want to unburden himself, I gave him my word I'd keep it to myself. But now, well, it's different. I think Elizabeth may have suspected something and that she believes he's got himself into a similar position now and that's why he's missing.'

If it was so, Norma Selby had no idea who the mystery woman might be.

DCI Roper sighed in exasperation, having checked nationally that there was no likely candidate on the missing persons list who fitted the description of the dead man, or who fitted as much of a description as they could come up with. He had insisted DC Gibbons continue with her inquiry because one corpse and one disappearance within a week added up to more than coincidence in his book. However, Superintendent Thorne, being aware of the continued lack of identification, might soon want to bring Brenda over to the murder team.

The pathologist had said that the injuries did not fit a pattern that was accidental but, conversely, the examination could not prove otherwise. What they did know for certain was that the body had been moved after death, which meant someone, somewhere, knew more than they were saying.

Doc Harris, as was his wont, called in after taking a routine blood sample from a suspected drunk/driving. Busy with his surgery and home visits, he only appeared at the station on such mundane chores or if a prisoner showed signs of illness. At the scene of sudden or suspicious deaths his duty was to pronounce extinction of life, no more than that. However, given his time over again he would have been a pathologist. Ian had pointed out that his little habit of drinking 'family-sized' whiskies might have been an impediment to travelling over a vast area. The Doc had retaliated by saying he might not have developed the habit in the first place. 'The dead', he said, 'are a lot less stress-inducing than the living.'

'Time you and Moira came over for dinner,' he said after tapping on Ian's door.

'Really? Is it company you're after or the low-down on the case?'

'Both, you cynic. Saturday?'

'I'm not sure. Can I –?'

'No, you can't. Saturday it is. I'll get Shirley to ring Moira. Make it about eight thirty. You can't work twenty-four hours a day, Ian. Not even you can do that.'

Before he could reply the Doc had gone.

He picked up the file and went to see Superintendent Thorne.

Twenty minutes later he collected Barry Swan from the control room as they were shortly due at the hospital mortuary. 'Mike Thorne is thinking along the same lines as us.'

'That these incidents are connected?'

'Yes.'

Barry did not reply. He was not so sure and he was vaguely worried by Ian's obsession that there was no such thing as coincidence: it could be leading them in the wrong direction.

They passed WPC Judy Robbins, hurrying somewhere with a sheaf of papers. The sight of her, to Ian, only acted as proof of his way of thinking. It seemed a lifetime ago that she babysat Mark

40

– ten, eleven years maybe? She must be pushing thirty and Lucy Swan would be the same age. Lucy, who had known Judy at school and was now Barry's wife. Look at the connections there, didn't it prove nothing and no one acted in isolation?

After the air-conditioned station house the heat outside enveloped them; a film of sweat shone on Ian's face before they reached the car which was thankfully parked in the shade of a tree.

The coroner, a local solicitor, under the directions of the Chief Constable, had appointed Gordon Grant as pathologist to perform the post-mortem. He was known to all and sundry as Quincy not only because he shared the same profession as that television character but also because he bore a remarkable resemblance to him physically. He was never addressed by this nickname and if he was aware of it he did not let on.

The victim's clothes and wrist-watch had been removed for forensic tests, the photographers snapping away as this was done. Barry, Ian noticed, was psyching himself up for the ordeal ahead. Hospitals he hated, although he could deal with casualties and death in far more unnatural places, but post-mortems he loathed and dreaded. His trick was not unknown to other members of CID whose duty it was to attend them. You simply faced the pathologist and his gruesome work-table but kept your eyes fixed on a point a foot or so above the scalpels and drills which he wielded. Everything he said as he worked could be heard but the business of the day was kept only in the periphery of vision. Ian made himself watch, convinced that one day it would become easier. So far it hadn't.

Methodically, Gordon Grant performed his task; fingernail clippings and scrapings bagged and labelled, an external examination, contusions and abrasions noted, the photographers homing in, taking close-ups; there was no averting the eyes for them. Rectal swabs, blood samples, incisions, stomach contents, bits from here, pieces from there and organs lying about then rinsed in water as Grant dissected them with the dispassion of a housewife preparing a casserole. And then it was over and the assistant was left to put the body back together again.

41

'I believe you gentlemen occasionally partake of something after such events?' Grant ripped off the rubber gloves and disposed of them, along with his protective clothing. 'I shan't be a minute.' He went off to shower. It was his last scheduled case for the day.

He returned in five minutes and unlocked a drawer in the obsolete filing cabinet which now served as a personal locker for mortuary staff as all the records were computerised. 'How appropriate.' He smiled his bland, professional smile. The whisky was Grants. It was an unwritten law that whoever finished a bottle replaced it. Last time it had been Bell's. It was another unwritten law that the hospital administration knew nothing about it either.

'As you saw, it's one of those cases where my findings can do little to assist you. The date of death is impossible to estimate, except within wide margins, and without knowing how long the body was exposed . . .' He shrugged. 'Well, you see what I'm getting at.'

The injuries were consistent with several heavy blows to the head but it was impossible to say whether they alone were the cause of death or whether early treatment might have saved the man's life.

'Who do we know with that MO?' Ian asked as they made their way back into Rickenham Green from the outskirts of the town where the huge hospital was situated.

'Can't think of anyone offhand.' Barry's face was still grey. The weapon was most likely that old favourite, a blunt instrument, possibly wooden – although the lack of flesh on the skull had made it difficult to find splinters – but a piece of piping, lagged, would have produced the same result.

'Jesus, someone must be missing him.'

'Yes, and if they are and they're not saying that suggests a lot, doesn't it?'

Barry ran a hand through his thinning, pale hair as he waited at a set of traffic lights then pulled the visor down against the glare of the sun. The shadowy reflections of the leaves of the horse chestnuts which lined Saxborough Road dappled over the bonnet of the car. With both side windows open they breathed in a mixture of diesel, fried onions, Chinese food and stale drains, the combination familiar in most towns in summer and somehow not as unpleasant as it should have been. 'Goddammit, this traffic doesn't improve.'

Barry enjoyed driving, a fact for which Ian was grateful as he did as little as possible himself, but he was not usually so impatient. More than the PM had upset him. Ian risked asking what it was.

'Lucy,' he said, two spots of colour appearing on his high cheekbones as he made the admission. 'Perhaps I'm being unfair but I had my fling before we were married. This is supposed to be different, no secrets.'

'Secrets?' This did not sound like the open, straightforward Lucy who was not afraid to speak her mind.

'She won't tell me where she went the other evening.'

'I shouldn't worry about it, you've nothing to fear from Lucy. She'll tell you in her own time.'

But Ian knew Barry did not like being on the receiving end of treatment he had dished out to many women over the years.

The coolness of the building was welcome when they returned.

'Press want a word,' DS Markham informed them when they updated themselves. Not that there was any new information.

Ian contacted Martyn Bright, editor of the *Rickenham Herald*, who was already aware of the suspicious death and had been promised some copy by that evening if it was to go in Friday's paper. It was a bland, uninformative statement which had to suffice, with an appeal for anyone with information as to the identity of the body to come forward. Bright lived up to his name. He realised at once there was no point in pushing, that what Ian Roper had told him was the extent of his knowledge.

Ian cut the connection then immediately dialled his home number to tell Moira to expect him around eight thirty to nine. He wanted to hear what DC Gibbons had to report before he went home.

Doodling on the blotter on his desk he thought it was virtually impossible for one man to disappear completely when so many people wished him to return and another to have been murdered without seeming to have been missed at all.

4

Carol Barnes had worked her way up through the department until she had reached the top. She was proud of her achievements and supposed an outsider would describe her as a career woman. Her reasons were obscure, even to herself, because she had never believed herself to be an ambitious person.

She had not married; there had been one or two opportunities, but her relationships with men usually ended in disaster. The fault lay with her. She was too demanding and slightly dominant with the men she really cared for and inclined to back off quickly from those who showed interest in her. Her instincts were more maternal than sexual and she would have made a far better mother than wife. It still wasn't too late but she was not holding her breath.

Working for the planning department of the local council she had been able to make doubly sure that the cottage she had bought as an investment was not in an area likely to be developed in the foreseeable future and that there were no road building plans. Where it was situated, it was highly unlikely there ever would be.

It lay midway between Rickenham Green and Frampton and although she had undertaken some modernisation it retained its character as a farm labourer's dwelling which meant it was by no means luxurious. Carol had originally purchased it as an investment but a slump in house prices had come at the wrong time, just as she was thinking of selling. Now she was not sorry because she had come to look upon it as home and the negative equity was no longer a problem as she had no intention of moving. She had begun to appreciate the peculiarities of the building and the solitude it provided and there was the added attraction that if the country ever got on its feet again she would be in an enviable position.

The cottage was constructed of stone, welcomingly cool in summer but difficult to heat in winter because she did not believe in central heating. Climbing roses and honeysuckle were tangled around the front porch, their stems gnarled with age. Carol left them as they were and they survived and flowered without any pruning. The back garden was also mostly untended but in that way retained its charm. Delphiniums, foxgloves and phlox seeded themselves and were interspersed with poppies and the occasional clump of barley. No contrived cottage garden could have been as lovely.

Three sides were bordered by fields, partly obscured by haw-thorn hedges, and at the front was a track which led to the B-road joining Rickenham to Frampton. Alongside the cottage was a narrow path which led to a dilapidated garage. Carol parked her car on the grass verge outside the front gate.

It was almost six when she returned home, although the time varied as she worked flexi-hours. The sun was beating down and heat rose from the hard-baked mud which formed the track. Life had taken an upward turn lately but she was too superstitious to think it could last and events were beginning to indicate that she had been right.

She planned what she would cook that night. It would be something simple, steak or some fish from the freezer, with salad as an accompaniment. To go with it there was wine. Salmon, she decided, as the Chablis which was in the fridge would be more appropriate for both the meal and the weather.

And tomorrow? Pasta tomorrow. She recognised what was happening, that she was trying to divert her thoughts from the real problems which threatened to engulf her.

If the weather remained as good she would make an early start, go in about seven and leave at lunchtime. She had several hours owing to her. It would be a perfect opportunity to get things sorted out once and for all.

Later, lying in bed, she knew she would not do it. Oh, yes, she might be at work before most of the others but it was tempting fate to initiate a discussion.

She lay awake for some time thinking about Nigel Pollock for no real reason other than that his name had cropped up several times lately, then she remembered the planning team meeting she was to attend in the afternoon. Sitting up she reset the alarm for a later time. There would be no chance of taking a half-day off.

'You think it could be that simple, that he's run off with somebody else's wife?'

'No, not quite that simple, sir. It's just a possibility based on something Norma Selby told me. But if that's what he has done there's no reason for him not to ring his family to say he's all right.'

'I take it you no longer believe he's dead?'

Brenda shrugged. 'I'm not sure what I think. I can't get Mrs Selby to open up about her husband, and it seems unlikely there's any connection. And suicide's still an option. I know there's been no sighting of Selby's car but it wouldn't be too difficult to find an isolated spot and perform the old trick with a length of hose and the exhaust or a bottle of pills.' She shook her head. The gleaming hair swung like silk. 'No, it doesn't ring true. From what I've learned of him he'd leave a note, there'd be some indication, and his family claim he was in good health and spirits the last time they saw him. Do you want me to continue, to see if there is a mystery woman?'

'The Super's hinting he'll want you working with me soon. Damnit all, I don't know if we're wasting our time or not. Yes, carry on for now. And thanks.'

Brenda Gibbons, cool and unflustered, departed for wherever it was she spent her time when she wasn't at work. Ian had no idea if there was a boyfriend or husband in the background but he had no curiosity about such matters.

47

The evening shift took over in the control room and, noticing it was already later than the time he'd given Moira, he too left. He was temporarily confused when he saw the Doc's Jaguar parked in Belmont Terrace. There was some talk of going over on Saturday night but this was Thursday. The house was empty. He went through the kitchen and found the three of them on what they called the patio but was really no more than two rows of paving slabs he and a neighbour had laid. Or, rather, Bob next door had set into sand because Ian was useless at practical things. There were drinks and bottles on the table. Ian kissed Moira then Shirley and raised his eyes inquiringly at the Doc.

'Not my doing, Ian. Moira insisted.'

How well his wife knew him. When he was tense and frustrated with the way things were going, the Doc was guaranteed to provide entertainment and help him relax in a way Moira couldn't because she was too close.

'I was hoping we could eat out here.' Moira looked doubtfully at the sky. A bank of cloud was building up in the west. There might even be a thunderstorm. For days it had been threatening.

'Know who he is yet?' the Doc asked when the women had gone in to see to the meal.

'Not a clue. And no way of finding out unless someone comes forward or the dental blokes get it right.'

'That'll do,' Shirley interrupted when she came out to tell them the food was on the table. Even she called her husband the Doc, Jim or James only when she was angry. She had recently undergone a hysterectomy and was still taking advantage of his solicitude. He smiled and held up his hands in surrender.

'Not another word, I promise,' he said, following her into the house.

Only when the Harrises had left and he was ready for bed did Ian allow his mind to dwell on the case, or cases. Random murders were rarer than most people believed, so what circumstances, what chain of events, had led to the death of the unidentified man?

48

DS Markham was investigating a series of arson attacks in the town. The first one had been on the premises of a television and video repair shop whose business was ailing and there was a suspicion it had been started deliberately for insurance purposes. The fire officer confirmed that a petrol-soaked rag had been pushed through the door and ignited, setting light to the tatty curtain behind it. It had happened when the man and his wife were out, which added to the suspicion. But their alibi was genuine and when there was a similar incident three days later the matter was taken more seriously. This was followed by a fire in the alley between Boots and Marks and Spencer when a pile of rubbish put out for collection the next morning was ignited. It looked as if they had a pyromaniac on their hands who needed to be stopped before someone was hurt.

Although Markham was supposed to be part of a team it did not always seem that way. Even on the rare occasions he socialised there was a barrier between himself and the people he was with, almost as if he resented being a member of the human race. He was also unusual in that he shunned patrol cars, preferring to travel on foot, to know exactly where he could find a villain or a petty criminal when he wanted him. Therefore he was on foot when he went to interview the owners of the corner shop in Railway Terrace where the most recent fire had taken place.

The shop sold everything; newspapers, confectionery, groceries, wines and spirits and a small selection of hardware. It served the remaining residents of the street and the area around the station which was under development. If they weathered the next couple of years the place would be a gold mine. The proprietors were young and not yet despondent. They were also suitably insured.

Angela Matthews wore her hair pulled severely back in a plait revealing a face which was neither plain nor pretty. Her pale blue overall hid whatever shape she might have. 'My husband's round the back,' she told Markham. 'He's still trying to clear up the mess before the glaziers get here. The loss adjuster's already been so we can go ahead.' A customer came in. 'Through that door. Can you find your own way?'

Markham surveyed the scene outside, which did not take long. The fire people had already inspected it, it was not that he had come for. He wanted information.

The yard was blackened and still damp from the hosepipes; one window which had shattered with the heat was boarded over. The brickwork and security door were undamaged.

'It's the last thing we needed,' Billy Matthews said. 'We were just beginning to make a go of it.' He shook his head. He was filthy, smuts and grime adhering to his clothes and streaking his face. 'Thank goodness we were properly insured.'

'You're not alone,' Markham said after offering a few words of sympathy. 'And we think it might be the same person or people responsible, unless you can think of a reason someone might want to make life difficult for you?'

'No. Me and the wife've discussed it. Everyone round here seems pleasant enough, and although we've got a couple of customers we allow to shop on credit, no one owes enough to want to put us out of business. Doesn't look like much, does it,' Matthews nodded towards the back wall of the property, 'but the stock room's smoke-damaged so we had to chuck out a fair bit of foodstuffs and it still stinks up in the flat.'

'You reported the fire yourself – did you see anyone around at the time?'

'No. We were on our way home and saw the smoke and rang from the phone in the car. We didn't risk going in. Strange, though, we rarely go out. We've got a boy of seven and he's autistic – it isn't easy to get anyone to mind him, but he stayed with my sister yesterday so we made the most of it and went out for a meal. If we'd been half an hour later things might've been different.'

'Did you pass another car?' Matthews was right, it was strange, the owners of the TV and video shop had also been out.

'No. Funny old area this, one half empty, the other half full of desirable properties.'

'If you do think of anything, give us a ring.' Markham handed him a card. The visit, as he had anticipated, had been a waste of time.

'What really pisses me off', Matthews continued as he pulled open the back gate to allow Markham through without dirtying his clothes, 'is that we had an offer for the shop a few months ago. We turned it down because this was our dream, our own little business. Besides, Sean's happy here and mixing with the customers is good for him. And my Angie's got a stubborn streak.' He grinned. 'This has only made her more determined to succeed.'

The back of the building had been in shadow but heat was already rising from the pavement in front and Angela Matthews was pulling down an awning to protect the goods in the window. On the opposite side the renovated properties had newly pointed brickwork and window boxes and tubs of flowers albeit chained to the wall. Paintwork was fresh, curtains were bright. Railway Terrace would one day be a sought-after address.

Neighbours had already been interviewed and all claimed the first they knew of the fire was when the tenders had arrived. No point then in questioning them again. He carried on on the same side of the road where one or two of the houses were boarded up. Already weeds had rooted in the guttering and a buddleia was sprouting between the wall and the paving stones. Markham paused. Mrs Mostyn lived here, the woman Sergeant Whitelaw had mentioned, but William Whitelaw was inclined to dramatise. Still, he was here, there was possibly a connection between the vandalism and the fire.

For some inexplicable reason old ladies liked Markham. Perhaps they sensed his apartness, like the child who is always alone in the playground, and their maternal instincts were aroused. But Markham was a loner by choice.

Mrs Mostyn opened the door and smiled. 'You're from the CID,' she said. 'I can tell by the jacket.'

Markham grinned. What they showed on television bore little

51

resemblance to the boring routine inquiries they had to deal with but he had to concede the point, detectives were frequently depicted clad in leather jackets. He wore his winter and summer, the thermostat in his hypothalamus unfailingly effective. Jeans, shirt, jacket in summer; jeans, T-shirt, shirt, jacket in winter, never a coat and never bare-armed.

'Come in, dear.'

It took a second or two to adjust to the dimness of the terraced house. The front room was neat, if old-fashioned, and there was a row of china ornaments on the mantelpiece, presents from her grandchildren. He expected to be offered a cup of tea but, like PC Mallet, was disappointed. Mrs Mostyn drank only milk or water or fruit juice.

'I've been told you believe these attacks to be personal, that somebody wants you out. Why would that be?'

She shrugged and looked around the room as if to remind herself she was still there. 'I don't know. But why isn't it happening to anybody else?'

'It does sometimes. And there was the fire at the shop.'

'Cars mostly, that's what they go for round here. Some of the people opposite have posh ones.'

'Have you any family?'

She looked up in surprise at the turn of the line of questioning. 'Yes, a daughter, she lives in Ipswich.'

'Does she visit?'

'Not as often as we'd both like. I'm too old to go far and although she's only in her fifties she suffers badly from arthritis, not so much trouble this time of year though. Oh, I see what you're getting at, young man. You think I'm some batty old dear with nothing better to do than waste police time. Is that it?'

'No. Carry on. You were telling me about your family.'

'My son-in-law drives her over whenever he can and my grandchildren are good, they visit too. But you needn't think any of them've got anything to do with it either. None of them have anything to gain. You know what it's like these days, you pay a stamp all your life, or my husband did, then when they think you can't cope they sell your house over your head to pay for your keep in a home. It's disgusting, it is. Welfare State indeed.' She cocked her head to one side and smiled cunningly. 'It isn't Di, they don't want me out. No point, she owns this house already.'

'But I thought –'

'Whatever you thought was wrong and you didn't think to ask. Some detective you are. I went to my solicitor some seven or eight years ago and got him to draw up an agreement. Di owns the house but it only becomes hers upon my death or if I do end up in some geriatric place. That way the thieving government can't get hold of it. And she doesn't want me to go into a home, she's forever insisting I go and live with them, not everyone's as lucky as me where family is concerned. The mortgage was all paid up when my husband died but whilst I'm here I'm responsible for the bills and the upkeep. It's all quite legal, you know, as long as you do it well in advance and not just before they cart you off in a strait-jacket.'

Markham guessed how much of a struggle the diminutive figure would put up if that unlikely event ever took place. 'In that case, Mrs Mostyn, what would anyone gain from wanting you out if you're no longer the freeholder?'

'Well, they don't know, do they? You didn't. And look at this area, all set for redevelopment. Do you know how much those houses opposite are going for? God knows where they get the money to buy them. Have you thought why the Matthews' place was set alight? They were out at the time, someone knew that. Same thing could be happening there.'

And Matthews had said he had received an offer for the business. There was no doubting Mrs Mostyn's sanity.

'Has anyone approached you, about buying your house?'

She was thoughtful. 'Yes, now you mention it. But it was ages ago. More than a year. Decent offer, too. I told him I wouldn't sell at any price, whatever this is worth is for my daughter's future.'

'Which estate agent was it?'

'None of them, as I recall. Some man came around. I didn't let him in, just said my piece on the doorstep.'

'Has he contacted you since?'

'No. I told him I didn't own the place, but I didn't say who did.'

'His name?'

'He didn't give it. He told me what the company was, but I'm blowed if I can remember now. So, what're you going to do about these hooligans?'

Very little, Markham suspected, because, apart from PC Mallet's suggestion of the presence of a patrol car at night, there was very little they could do. He took his leave and decided it was worth checking at the Town Hall. There might be some substance to what Mrs Mostyn had said about her property and the shop. He had not heard of any immediate development plans but it was worth a try and if there was a compulsory purchase order the council would not be sending someone round to frighten her.

It was Carol Barnes Markham spoke to.

'Get him some tea or something, I'll be down in a minute,' Barry Swan said into the internal telephone. He was in the middle of a conversation with DC Gibbons as to what number 3 squad had come up with. They were responsible for follow-up inquiries, which was ludicrous as there was nothing to follow up apart from two people who admitted being in the vicinity of the river between Thursday and Tuesday. They were sticking to Thursday as a starting point because that was the night of Selby's disappearance. Barry had just received a call saying another woman had remembered something.

'I'm sorry, my mother-in-law was taken ill on Sunday and I didn't think any more about it until today. I was there, with my children, on Saturday afternoon. We took a picnic because my husband was watching cricket and we didn't want to go with him.'

'What time was this?'

'We got there about three and stayed until five. Only near the bridge, though. It's a bit creepy in the woods and you hear so many awful things. There was an argument, you see.'

'An argument?' Was this it, the missing link?

'I heard voices, one was male, he was shouting but I couldn't hear the replies. Anyway, the children were making enough noise and I was worried about Ben falling in the river. They must have been just inside the wood because I didn't see them. Be quiet!' she said in a louder voice, addressing one of her children. 'Sorry. Do you need me to come down to the police station?'

'If you wouldn't mind. Meanwhile, it would be helpful if you could try and remember anything that you did hear. Exactly what was said, even if it was only a sentence. And thank you very much for ringing.'

DC Gibbons had raised her eyebrows.

'Might mean something. It all seems to be happening at once, there's someone else downstairs wanting to talk to us.'

'Well, it's given number 3 squad something to do,' Brenda said. 'And if what that woman said is true then there were other people there who have not come forward.'

What have we here? Barry thought when he saw Sebastian Roberts seated patiently in an interview room studying his clean nails. He did not know how he knew but he was certain Mr Roberts was homosexual. Maybe there was an aura about them which they themselves also recognised and this was why there were so few instances of them approaching men who were not of the same sexual orientation.

'Chief Inspector?' Sebastian stood politely when Barry entered the room.

'No, I'm Sergeant Swan.' He indicated the chair and they both sat down.

'I've had a few minutes to think about it and I've got a feeling I might be wasting your time.'

'You can let me be the judge of that.' Barry would have been mortified had someone told him the words and tone were an exact mimicry of DCI Roper.

Sebastian took a sip of the coffee with which he had been provided and prayed he was doing the right thing. 'It's a friend of mine, well, an acquaintance really. A customer. Charles

Carlos. He comes into my pub quite a bit but he hasn't been in for over a week now.'

It fell into place. 'The Pink Elephant? Your pub?'

'Yes. Sorry, I should've explained. Chaz, Mr Carlos, has been a bit depressed lately. Boyfriend trouble.' He paused, gauging the detective sergeant's reaction. There wasn't one.

'A row?'

'More a parting of the ways. They'd been together some time. Chaz took it badly.'

'And you think he may have harmed himself?' He did not want to put words into Roberts's mouth. This Carlos character may have killed his lover in rage or jealousy. The lover, therefore, might be the victim.

'You can never be sure, can you? But I don't think he's the type. It's daft, but I keep thinking about the poor man you found whose name you don't know and, well, not seeing Chaz . . .' He left the sentence unfinished.

'And you think it might be Mr Carlos?'

'Can I ask you something? I didn't hear it on the radio but my customers are saying it's a suspicious death, does that mean murder?'

'We're inclined to think so.'

'As soon as I heard I tried to ring Chaz but there's no answer from his flat.' Sebastian paused. 'He can't have been murdered.'

He looked genuinely puzzled but Barry knew people always assumed murder was what happened to other people, never anyone they knew.

'Do you have his address, Mr Roberts?'

'No, only the telephone number. Oh dear. He's about that age, you see, mid-thirties.' He pressed his thumb and forefinger against his temples in a rather dramatic gesture of despair.

'His friends?'

'I'm not sure. He spoke to most people in the pub but I don't think any of them were particular friends.'

'The boyfriend?'

'I don't know him, I don't even know his name.'

Barry made a note of Charles Carlos's telephone number and advised Sebastian that he would be sending someone round to interview his customers. He realised it was the last thing he needed when he was just starting out but that could not be helped.

Carlos's number was local. It would not be difficult to find the address. Barry then thanked him. He did not add that the majority of cases were not solved by pure detection work but by the public coming forward with information. His hand shook in anticipation as he dialled the number he had been given. There was no reply.

Now number 2 squad also had something to work on. Find where Carlos lived then go round there and interview the neighbours. At last initial inquiries of some substance would be underway. If Carlos was the man. Too bad if he, too, had simply decided to disappear.

Unlike a killing in a domestic setting this case had no base from which to begin. An unidentified body in a wood, no papers, no nothing on his person and no forensic evidence in the vicinity: therefore no starting place. But now, well, hopefully, things would move forward.

Barry took this new information down to the control room. What he lacked in height he made up for with stylish dressing and a slightly swaggering walk; the thinning hair on top he made up for by growing the back longer over his collar. He ran a hand through it now, an oft-repeated action which may have been the cause of the thinness or an attempt to ensure what hair there was disguised it. He was dressed in beige slacks and a shirt which was fashionably loose, as were the jackets he favoured and which caused Ian to make remarks along the lines that he was too old to grow into them now.

British Telecom obliged and came up with the name and address of the subscriber of the relevant number. Mr Charles Carlos had taken over the rental just under a year ago and paid his bills on time. His number was due to be listed in the next directory. Privilege indeed, the public were no longer supplied with addresses.

WPC Robbins and PC Green were in the nearest patrol car. They had to play it softly. Carlos might be sitting at home nursing a broken heart not lying in the freezer down at the mortuary. 'Here. Pull in here,' Judy said.

There was no answer from Carlos's basement flat and the door was locked. Judy Robbins climbed the steps to the front door of the house which was on street level. A harassed-looking woman answered the door and said she couldn't help. Chaz was a tenant, he paid his rent and kept to himself, it was not her job to keep a record of his movements.

'Do you have a spare key?'

'Why? Want to snoop around, do you?' The woman, who had not volunteered her name, brushed back her lank hair.

'When did you last see your tenant?'

'Dunno. About a week ago, I suppose.'

'No one else has seen him recently either.' Judy waited for the penny to drop.

'You mean he's done a bunk? Left me without no rent?'

'I wasn't necessarily thinking that.'

'Hasn't it occurred to you he might be ill? Or worse?' PC Green added.

'God, I'd never let the place again if anything's happened to him in there.'

'We'd better have a look then, hadn't we?'

Begrudgingly she went to fetch the key and let them in. Her name turned out to be Helena, a pretty name for a plain, thin woman. Helena stood in the doorway, refusing to go in while they looked around. The flat was musty and airless and a bluebottle battered itself against the window having followed them in. All was clean and tidy and there was no sign of the occupant.

The two PCs opened drawers and cupboards. Charles Carlos possessed an expensive CD player, a television set and video recorder, some decent clothes and very little else. The flat was furnished and Helena said apart from those items everything else belonged to her. She cheered up and decided to be more

58

helpful once she knew there was not a dead body beneath her own floorboards.

'I suppose he must work,' she said, 'but I can't say he ever told me where. He's out a lot in the day, and most evenings really. It's strange I haven't seen him for so long. Still, he pays his rent monthly and it's not due yet.'

In answer to PC Green's question she continued, 'Can't say I've noticed many friends. Just the one really. Pale young man, looks ill to me.'

'Well,' Judy said once they were back in the car, 'for a woman who claims she doesn't keep a record of her tenant's movements, she certainly seemed to notice a lot.' She picked up the radio and passed on the information to headquarters.

'For God's sake, why not?'

'Sorry. I just didn't think of it.' There was a tinge of colour across Barry's high cheekbones. He had forgotten to ask a very basic question.

Ian was not as annoyed as he sounded, he knew too well that the less there was to work on the more likely it was mistakes were made. Both of them functioned better under stress when there were numerous witnesses and several leads. But if Charles Carlos had not been seen since Thursday either, surely a description of what he was wearing was the obvious thing to ask for.

'Get someone to find out.'

DC Gibbons was going back to Carlos's flat between six and seven in case he had returned. If he was not there they would need to start looking for the next of kin to see if he had contacted them recently or they knew of his whereabouts.

'Markham's going to Roberts's place,' Barry said. Both Roberts and Helena had last seen Carlos on Thursday.

'OK, make sure he finds out.' It had crossed his mind to get Roberts to ID the body but he decided to give it a few more hours. 'Where is he now?'

59

'Markham? Typing something up at his desk when I last saw him.'

'The arson thing, I suppose. Well, he's not averse to a pint, no doubt he'll make the most of it.'

Carol Barnes poured a generous measure of gin and tonic and added a slice of lemon and a handful of ice-cubes which chinked against the lead crystal as she carried the glass out to the garden. Her life had not been easy, all she had gained she had had to work for, and the team meeting had left her with a vague headache behind her eyes. 'Oh, well,' she muttered, 'this'll kill or cure.' She sipped the gin, dubious of its effects. She was aware that too much made her depressed. But wasn't she already depressed? If only she could talk, really talk, then she would at least know where she stood.

Outside was a folding chair, one that when extended fully became a sun-lounger. She strolled towards it with a smile on her face.

At thirty-five she looked forty but she had what her mother used to describe as good bones. Old age would be kind to her. She was on the tall side but this did not prevent her from holding herself well and wearing her dark hair, lightly streaked with grey, on top of her head. Her glasses, which hung from a chain around her neck when not in use, were framed in mannish rectangular tortoiseshell plastic but she knew they added gravitas because her position as a female in charge of mostly males was not always enviable. When she removed them her face was softer.

What was Nigel Pollock up to? She had had many dealings with him over the past years and although she had her suspicions that he had not started out strictly on the side of the law that was certainly not the case now.

There were too many things she did not understand at the moment, and not having a television set meant she was unaware the police were trying to trace the whereabouts of Bruce Selby. As she only listened to Radio 4 or classical music from her vast collection of cassettes, which she could slot into the pocket of the portable radio, she did not know that an appeal had been launched for him to come forward.

Earlier that day she had received a visit from the police. It had set her thinking. She considered herself to be a fairly good judge of character, maybe she was wrong about Nigel Pollock. She had been certain he had stopped entertaining ideas of developing Railway Terrace years ago. Besides, one side of the street was in the process of being renovated.

'I'd better see to the meal,' she said, carrying her empty glass inside.

Carol took lamb chops from the fridge and placed them on the rack of the grill pan before preparing runner beans. If she spent more time on the garden, she thought, she might start growing her own. She switched on the radio. She frowned. It was tuned to the local channel but the news was just starting. The headlines spoke of overseas conflicts; this was followed by an item describing how a fishing boat out of Lowestoft had picked up a mine in its nets. A child was going to receive an award for bravery for rescuing his friend from drowning. The recent murder she had been hearing about was relegated to fourth place. 'Police are still trying to confirm the identity of the man whose body was discovered on the outskirts of Rickenham Green on Tuesday. Anyone who was in the vicinity of the bridge or the river during the preceding five days is requested to come forward. All information will be treated in confidence.'

Carol slid a runner bean through the slicer. 'Surely someone must know who he is.' She thought perhaps he had no friends or relatives. Of course, someone had to know him, whoever it was that had killed him, and he was unlikely to come forward.

That there was possibly an undetected murderer somewhere in the vicinity did not worry Carol. She was security conscious and did not take unnecessary risks, apart from which she truly believed that there was always a justifiable reason for someone to get themselves killed, barring accidents. She did not discount the possibility of a completely random murder but was sensible enough to realise that if, in the middle of the night, someone unknown to her broke in and ended her life, there was nothing she could do about it; life was too short anyway to worry about the remoteness of such an event.

She turned on the grill, placed the beans in a saucepan and added salt and, feeling idle, opened a tin of new potatoes. The news item continued. A description of what the dead man had been wearing followed.

'If you think you know, or know of, this man, please contact your nearest police station to enable us to make a positive identification.' Us? She had missed a bit. The last words were obviously recorded by a police spokesman.

She thought about it. It was cleverly done. Yesterday the news had talked about an unidentified male; today they were using words such as 'confirming identification' and 'making a positive identification'. To her mind it meant they were making further progress than they wished the public to believe.

The potatoes were simmering and the chops were beginning to hiss. Carol added boiling water to the beans then sat down to think. The conclusion she came to was unbearable and therefore not one to be contemplated. It was another facet of the way her life was changing that needed to be stored at the back of her mind.

I'm a coward, she decided. Tomorrow, without fail, she would ask some of the questions that she should have asked initially. Mentally she prepared herself to live with the answers, whatever they might be.

5

Nigel Pollock bent rules and manipulated people for his own ends but he was not actually a crook and his success had put an end to the shady deals he was once part of.

He sat opposite Anne-Marie and listened to her account of the day and what the children had done. They were in bed now, having had tea earlier. The adult Pollocks preferred to eat together later. My wife, he thought, as he watched her talking, is sexier when she's in jeans and unmade-up. And he had to give her due credit, she was not the sort of woman to want to live up to and beyond their means, nor did she see the need for an au pair or a nanny when she was at home all day herself. Nigel loved his family so fought off – mostly – the advances of other women who were attracted more by the power he exuded than his looks. He was heavy-framed, bull-necked and flat-featured with little distinction between the planes of his face, but he carried no extra weight and he dressed well.

'Coffee?' Anne-Marie stacked the used crockery.

'Please.'

She knew by the way he was looking at her that he was about to say he had to go out. It didn't matter, they spent a lot of time together.

'I won't be very long. Look, fix up a babysitter for tomorrow and we'll go out for a meal.'

Nigel drank his coffee quickly then left. He wanted to speak to Leon, he felt there was something wrong, it was unlike Chaz not to be on the scene no matter what his personal problems. And there was that unidentified body. Chaz was trouble, he had guessed that from the first time he met him and he had tried to inveigle his way into Nigel's circle.

The BMW glided smoothly through the gates, windows closed, air-conditioning on. Despite the humidity Nigel wore a jacket and tie, it was his uniform, it made him stand out from the jeans and T-shirt or short-sleeved shirt brigade of fellow businessmen who liked to consider themselves as trendy and youthful. Pollock was nearing fifty but age meant nothing to him as long as life was good.

Leon Dawson stood at the bar with half a pint of lager and his usual grim expression. Nigel wondered if he was capable of stretching his lips into a smile. 'Refill?'

'No, ta.'

'Pint for me, please, Sebastian, I've got the car tonight.' He paid for his drink and Sebastian walked to the other end of the counter and started wiping it unnecessarily. 'What's up with him tonight?'

Leon shrugged. 'No idea.'

It was unlike Sebastian to be anything other than chatty and friendly to every customer, known or otherwise. 'Leon, where's Chaz?'

'I don't know. I haven't seen him since last week.' He paused. Like Pollock and Roberts, Leon believed the dead man might well be Chaz, but there was no point in getting involved with the police for a little runt like that. Especially after what he had discovered.

'If you know anything, it's best if you tell me. Look, Chaz hasn't been seen for a week and Bruce Selby's missing and not responding to requests to make himself known to the police.' Was it possible they were all up to something behind his back? It was doubtful, Chaz and Leon didn't have the brains and Selby didn't have the guts. A sixth sense told him Leon was not lying. He left as Markham walked in.

Leon remained where he was, making his drink last because he always liked to be in control. He had seen what alcohol could do to Chaz who was also a liar and had a dirty mouth. Leon knew no more than Pollock but he guessed that Bruce Selby, somehow realising Chaz had been murdered, had gone into hiding because of that photograph.

'Oh, my!' Brenda Gibbons jumped when the first clap of thunder rent the air without warning. The sky had blackened in seconds, there was a flash of lightning, a sound like the roll of heavenly drums then a bang. The rain followed almost immediately, bouncing off the bonnet of the car and filling the air with the smell of warm, wet tarmac. No wonder I've got a headache, she thought as she headed towards Charles Carlos's address. There was still no reply, nor any from the house above although Brenda was sure she had seen the curtain move.

Markham stepped inside the Pink Elephant and almost did a double take. Was this once the Prince William? Even the bar was in a different place. He had heard it was doing a good trade but there were only seven or eight people there. 'Sebastian Roberts?' Markham showed his identity without making it obvious to the other customers.

'Yes. They said someone would be coming.'

'A couple more questions about Mr Carlos and then if you'd tell me if any of these people are locals I'd like to have a word with them.' He continued speaking without looking round. 'And I'll have a pint of lager, please.'

Sebastian took his money which pleased Markham. Too many men in business surreptitiously offered perks or tried to curry favour. 'You saw Mr Carlos last Thursday, can you remember what he was wearing?'

'Jeans.' He paused. That was easy, he always did. 'Yes, and a black T-shirt. I remember because it had the names of towns where some band or other had been on tour. I meant to look at it later to see which one.'

'No jacket or coat?'

'In this weather? Oh.' Sebastian was suddenly aware of Markham's leather jacket. 'Actually, now you mention it, he did. One similar to yours. I saw him take if off the pegs there before he went out to the Gents.' He pointed to a row of brass hooks to the right of the bar. 'That was the last time I saw him.'

'He went out through there?'

'Yes.'

Between the bar and the coat hooks was a door and a sign for the toilets. Markham opened it and found himself in a narrow passage, completely disorientated after the old days. On the left was another door, marked Private, which led to the living accommodation upstairs; the two doors to the right were male and female lavatories. He decided to make use of the facilities, which were clean, the walls tiled and with vents rather than windows.

'Do people use the back entrance?' Markham asked when he returned to the bar.

'Sometimes. If they need a pee before they go and especially if the bar's crowded. And it was that night. When I last saw Chaz, that is.'

Helena Maddern had seen her tenant on the Thursday morning, he had been in the Elephant that evening, so how many other people had seen him, had been in a position to see him leave by the back way?

'And the boyfriend? Was he here?'

'No. He works shifts. Of course, that roadhouse. What's it called? The Coach and Horses? Something like that anyway. I should've mentioned it to Sergeant Swan but it's only just occurred to me.'

Nerves, Markham thought. It was far easier to recall facts on your own territory. 'Anyone here who was here that night?'

'Leon Dawson, at the end of the bar. The others? I can't say but I doubt it. You'd need to come back on one of our music nights to catch them all.'

'Thanks.'

He walked casually up to Leon and introduced himself. 'I believe you know Charles Carlos.' Still the present tense, until they were certain.

'I do.'

Markham established that he too had last seen him on that Thursday.

'Is it him, the body that was found?'

'Would you care to come and identify it?'

'No thanks. No skin off my nose whether he's dead or alive.'

'Oh?'

'Slimy little scumbag.'

'Would you care to elucidate?'

'No. Let's just say I can't stand him but if it is him, it wouldn't surprise me.'

'Plenty of people wanting to kill him?' Still the present tense. Leon was using it also.

'I expect so.' And that was the extent of the interview with Dawson, who refused to be drawn further. Markham made a note of his address. No point in being too awkward just yet; if it became necessary later, there was no one better than himself in making things uncomfortable.

'You don't happen to know the name of Mr Carlos's boy-friend?'

'Yeah. Martin. Don't know the surname.'

'Cheers. You've been very helpful.'

It meant taking a car because the place to which Roberts had referred was five miles out of Rickenham Green. It was called the Stag and Hounds. There was a large car-park and the front had been mocked up to appear Tudor. Inside were the requisite number of horse brasses.

The staff seemed to be composed of bored-looking youngsters; perhaps, Markham thought, their environment had had this effect. A blank-faced girl asked if he was eating because most of the tables were full and there were bookings waiting.

'Is Martin working this evening?' He could have telephoned

but he did not want to give him a chance to flee or think up a story.

'I dunno. Who's asking?' She stood behind a small table, responsible for taking bookings and showing people to their tables. If she did not know who else was on duty she must switch off her brain at work.

'I do.' Markham showed her his identity. She was suitably unimpressed.

'You'll have to ask the manager, I can't leave my station.'

Markham's smile would have done credit to an East End bouncer. The time for courtesy had passed. 'Get him then.'

The girl's eyes widened but she did not argue.

The manager was more obliging and said that he could borrow his office to speak to Martin but that he did not believe the boy could be in any kind of trouble. 'He waits on tables or helps wherever necessary. He's reliable and honest,' he volunteered before going to find him.

Martin Cook was not a prepossessing sight and did not seem capable of having the strength to carry a loaded tray. Thin and pale, a small scar on the side of his mouth, eyebrows and hair albino light, it was difficult to imagine what Charles Carlos had seen in him. He took Markham by surprise by shaking his hand. There was a bright blue sticking plaster on his thumb. But when he spoke his voice was deep and confident and he did not flinch from making eye contact. The lank hair was probably due to the greasy atmosphere of the kitchen where, according to the menu he had scanned while he waited, everything was apparently cooked in a 'coating of seasoned breadcrumbs and deep fried', apart from the steak, which probably came from a different frozen food manufacturer.

'A week ago Wednesday,' Cook said. 'I haven't tried to contact him since. It's best. We both knew it was over for a while but neither of us knew how to end it. Too many arguments and, well, there were other men, I'm sure.' Redness crept up his face. 'He started making fun of my job. It's not much, I know, but it's a living wage and I get food and transport home.'

'So where's Chaz now?'

'Now? He could be anywhere.' The reaction was genuine, it had not crossed Martin Cook's mind that his friend was doing anything other than carrying on as he had before.

'Where does he work?'

'He doesn't, he's unemployed.'

'But?' Markham had not missed the quick frown.

'He's never short of money, well, not like I am. Is he in trouble, sir?'

'He could be in real trouble.' Markham took a chance. He had summed up Martin Cook and not found him wanting. He was the sort who, if he knew or suspected something, would have come forward; either he had nothing to hide or he had been to RADA. 'Martin, you know we're investigating a murder . . .'

The boy's face went grey and he crumpled, staggering backwards into a chair. 'Oh, no. You don't mean Chaz.'

'Does he have any relatives?'

'What? No. I mean, not here. Parents somewhere or other.'

'Would you be prepared to come with me, to identify the body?'

Martin took a deep breath. 'Yes, I'll do it. I don't suppose anyone else will.'

Markham squared things with the manager and drove back to town, having asked for the mortuary to be alerted to prepare the body for viewing.

Martin Cook failed to hold back the tears when he saw the clothes Charles Carlos had been wearing when he was killed. By the time they reached the hospital he was more composed and took both Markham and the mortuary assistant by surprise when he gently stroked the arm of the victim.

'No.' The assistant grabbed his arm as he reached for the sheet which covered his face. 'No,' he repeated. 'That's not necessary, not now you've identified him.'

It had not been difficult, Cook and Carlos had shared a sexual relationship for a long time, he had known immediately, had probably known as soon as he was shown the leather jacket.

69

Cook's alibi for that Thursday was a twelve-hour shift which he had offered to work to keep his mind off the final separation of the previous night. They would check, of course, but no one knew when Carlos had been killed therefore it was necessary to have an alibi for every minute of every day since. 'I've still got his door key.' Cook removed it from a ring and handed it to Markham. 'I forgot to give it to him. I knew I wasn't going to need it again, but . . .' But he hadn't expected their parting to be so final.

Cook made a statement back at the station. Markham was pensive. Cook had been in possession of a key, he might not be strong but he could have used the element of surprise, going in when Carlos was asleep, maybe because his version of events was not correct – maybe Carlos had ditched him or found someone else. That would leave the problem of the disposal of the body. He could not have moved it alone and he claimed he had no transport. No, something told Markham Cook was not involved.

Ian was already asleep when the telephone rang. He groaned automatically before going downstairs to answer it. There was no bedside extension because Moira slept more heavily than Ian and this way she was not disturbed.

'Roper,' he said abruptly.

'We just thought you'd want to know we've got an ID, sir.' It was DC Gibbons, still at the station at eleven thirty.

'Good. I'll be in early.' It was a start. Now they could build up a picture of the man. He yawned and went straight back to sleep, the night shift could get on with it.

'Didn't you hear the phone?'

'You know I never do,' Moira replied as she made toast the following morning. 'I sleep like a log. Clear conscience.'

'What's that supposed to mean?'

'Don't be bad-tempered, darling.' She smiled sweetly and he rubbed his bristled chin, envious of her ability to look good first thing in the morning. 'It's obvious where Mark gets it from.'

'He's got no excuse. I'd be fine if I slept twelve hours every night.'

Moira did not point out that he usually managed the recommended eight, sometimes longer at weekends, and allowed his grumbling to go over her head. Their son would be home in just over a week and, from the conversation during their last telephone call, she suspected he was working round to asking if Lara could stay too. She was sure they were sleeping together but no matter how liberal-minded Ian thought himself to be she knew he would not allow them to share a bedroom under his roof. It was only at such times that their age difference was noticeable and it meant clearing out the box room and getting the folding bed down from the attic.

Ian left early and she stood at the sink admiring the garden. The thunderstorm had revived the wilting plants in a way no amount of watering from a can could do. The sun was warm again but there were still a few drops of moisture on the taller shoots of grass which always sprang up in the middle of the lawn. The coffee maker gurgled and spluttered. Moira took a mugful out to the back and enjoyed a few minutes' peace before work.

There had been no further incidents of arson and Markham was required to join Ian's team. However, unsatisfied with the offhand manner in which Carol Barnes had treated his questions, he decided, in his lunch break, to pay her another visit, taking a chance that her flexi-hours meant she was in. He stated his business to one of the females behind the reception desk and was told to use the internal telephone and given a three-digit number. In less than two minutes he was shown up to Carol's office.

She was too thin for Markham's taste but chicly dressed in a cream button-through outfit. Her hair was in a French pleat and her green eyes were enhanced by the lenses of her glasses. 'Again?' she said.

71

'Yes.' He hoped to ruffle her because he was certain she was hiding something. 'You say no one's interested in the east side of Railway Terrace, that no development plans have been proposed?'

'That's correct.'

'I have information it might be otherwise.'

'You do? It's news to me. As I told you before, I'm head of the planning department.' She stood up and went over to a filing cabinet rather than tapping into her desk-top terminal. Markham wondered if it was to give herself time to think.

'No, look, you can see for yourself. If it's any help there was a tentative approach by one of the superstore giants but the proposition was unfeasible.' She spread open a photocopied map of that area. 'See? New access roads would have had to be built and that couldn't be done without knocking down rows of properties in good repair or bridging the railway line. An underpass is also out of the question because geological reports show the terrain is unsuitable for tunnelling. May I ask why you need to know all this?'

'Curiosity.'

'Oh!' Carol Barnes was disconcerted, possibly affronted, but he had not rattled her. At least he was convinced some dubious firm was not using strong-arm tactics to persuade property owners to sell. Initially he had not liked the woman, finding her cold. Now he realised she was merely professional and had probably struggled to get to the top, and although she had said the young man who had shown him up was one of her team, he doubted whether Carol Barnes could ever be any more part of a team than himself. He grinned as he descended the stairs two at a time.

DC Gibbons leant against the back of a chair, arms folded, ankles crossed, as she listened to the morning's briefing. Although she was involved in the murder of Charles Carlos the word had not come from Superintendent Thorne that she was officially off the Selby case. She suspected this was deliberate, that it was intended she continue making inquiries as and when she could. The Chief had hinted it might be an idea to find Patti Evans, the woman with whom he was, according to his sister-in-law, having an affair some years previously. Most likely it would be a wild-goose chase but she might be able to give a bit more insight into his character. Eight days and still no sign of the man.

Two detectives on the night shift had returned to Carlos's flat with a search warrant in case the landlady was unhelpful. It was not necessary; she let them in and watched as they went through his possessions bit by bit. Financial papers related only to what Martin Cook had told them, that Chaz was unemployed, but there were several personal letters through which they were able to contact his parents. They lived in Bristol and were travelling up that day, still, according to the officer who spoke to them, unaware of their son's habits and lifestyle since he had left home.

It did not take DC Gibbons long to find Mrs Patti Evans, simply because she knew, from what Norma Selby said, that she and her husband lived in a specially designed bungalow. All the Evanses who lived in streets she knew could be ruled out, which only left four others. It was third time lucky and she rang to make an appointment to see her after she had interviewed the barmaid from the Pink Elephant.

Brenda, a careful driver, pulled into the kerb outside the sprawling bungalow, the wheels of the car perfectly aligned. She had none of the aggression of some drivers who knew they were good, but was content to be in possession of a certificate which stated she had passed her advanced driving test. Her small achievements were always personal, her temperament such that she did not need to prove anything to anyone else. She had already done that: her whole existence had shown what she called the breed of coddling experts to be wrong. An alcoholic, divorced mother, finally foster parents, and inner-city schooling had done nothing to blunt her determination to succeed. Of course, she had to accept that she was lucky in her foster parents and that her teachers had not all succumbed to the fatigue of trying to control, rather than educate their pupils. Her

73

philosophy was that no one should blame someone else for their own inadequacies, which did not go down too well with some of the agencies with whom she came into contact.

Her only mistake had been Harry. She thought of him now as she approached the Evanses' place but only because his dream had been to own a bunglow; one of their many differences, Brenda was never comfortable sleeping on ground level.

It was not an exceptional building from the outside but it had not yet had the chance to weather. It was well constructed, the layout pleasing and the garden just beginning to mature, and she saw how pleasant it would be in a few years' time. If you liked bungalows. Little upkeep would be required for doors and windows as they were double glazed and framed in some sort of white PVC. At the side was parked a battered Ford Escort.

A woman of no more than five feet opened the door. Her eyes flickered up and down, taking in the long-haired female with the open, healthy face, the tan skirt and cream blouse. 'Yes?' she said a little uncertainly.

'DC Gibbons, Brenda Gibbons.' She produced her identity. 'Mrs Patti Evans?' In turn she made a quick physical assessment: short, thirty-five-ish, rounded but not plump, pretty but tired. Tired of what? She was in shorts and a cotton top and her bare feet were as dirty as her hands.

'Of course. I didn't realise it was that time already. Come in, please.'

Brenda followed her down the extra wide, tiled hallway which divided the property in two and led straight to the back garden. There were crumbs of dry earth along its length. 'In here,' Patti Evans said, pushing open the wide door. 'Excuse me for a minute, I'll just wash this lot off.'

While she was removing the soil from her extremities Brenda stood by the open glass doors and surveyed the garden. There was a trowel, a small fork and a plastic carrier full of weeds on the lawn beside a border; the plants were in muted shades of blue and purple and peach, interspersed with white. Much thought had gone into the planning and layout. The room itself

74

was immaculate and light and airy although it held little furniture and no signs of real living. The lack of books, ornaments and photographs gave it the appearance of a show house rather than somewhere where people spent their lives together. Perhaps the Evanses wanted no reminders of their other life before the accident.

In front of the television was an adjustable chair, one arm swung out in readiness for when Mr Evans wanted to slide into it from his wheelchair. There was no sound of the man himself, only of running water.

'Sorry about that. I always weed barefoot, I like the feel of the soil. Would you like some tea?'

'No thanks. You're probably wondering why I'm here. It's a long shot but we're making inquiries about a man named Bruce Selby who has disappeared. Someone suggested you once knew him.'

Patti Evans's face registered bewilderment before she flushed. 'Yes. I heard on the television.'

'Is your husband in?'

'Gareth? No, why? Did you want to speak to him?'

'No. I didn't want to cause you any embarrassment.'

'Oh.' She was flustered but grateful. 'He's at the physio's, he still goes twice a week. I collect him later. What did you want to know about Bruce?'

'How did you meet him?'

'It was just after the accident. Gareth was in hospital, he'd been there some time and we knew he'd never walk again. I was approached by a local firm who offered to buy our house – we couldn't have stayed there, not with a wheelchair – and build this,' she waved a hand, 'at a ridiculously cheap price. We thought there was a catch at first, but they simply wanted to use it as a show-place for others like it and we agreed. Our part of the bargain was that they could bring people here but only for a year.' She grinned ruefully. 'I suppose it was better publicity having a real cripple to show how efficient it all was. We've been here eight years now.'

'Mrs Evans, I don't understand how Mr Selby was involved.'

'It was only indirectly. I think he was something to do with the planning department, then he came to survey everything before we moved in. He was kind to me, very understanding.' She gripped her hands together. 'It should never have happened. Please don't think it was his fault. I was at my lowest ebb, miserable and lonely and worried sick about Gareth and how we'd cope. And after all those months, a year, in fact, sexually frustrated. It's no excuse and I've never repeated it. I have had', she said with some stoicism, 'to learn to live with it.'

'When did you last see him?'

'Not since Gareth came out of hospital. I've no idea where he is now. Miss . . . er, I'm not sure what to call you.'

'Brenda will do.'

'Well, Brenda, then. I have to collect Gareth now. Will you need to speak to me again?'

'It's very unlikely. But if we do, I'll telephone first.' Without saying so, Brenda implicitly let Patti Evans know her husband would not be made aware of her indiscretion.

6

Somewhere, many generations ago, a foreigner may have been responsible for the name Carlos but no one in the family knew or had bothered to find out. As far as they were concerned they were British and proud of it. 'Charles was different,' a tearful Doreen Carlos told DCI Roper. 'He was what you'd call romantic, as a kid he used to pretend we had a mysterious background, he even told his school friends we were gypsies.'

'When did you last see him, Mrs Carlos?'

'Two years ago. We never lost touch, though, he was a good boy that way. He'd write; sometimes, he'd forget to put his new address on his letters, but he always let us know he was safe and well. I thought when he moved here he'd settled down. We never even saw his flat but me and Derek didn't like to interfere, we were the same with the girls, weren't we, Dad?'

Derek Carlos nodded. Used to his wife doing all the talking, he was content to let her take control.

'My next question might be . . .' Ian searched for the right word and could not find it, 'distressing' was what he said. 'Did you know your son was homosexual?'

'No.' It was Mr Carlos who answered. His wife put a handkerchief to her lips and held it there, perhaps to prevent herself from speaking.

'Yes.' She spoke quietly to the man who wished it was not so. 'Yes, we did, Dad. He never told us but we discussed it. There were never any girlfriends, you see.' She turned back to Ian. 'He *was* different, we always knew that and we sort of put two and two together. I'd accepted it. That's why we didn't push him, about visiting or anything. You see, it was Charles who couldn't bear for us to know.'

Another hour passed and Ian was no wiser. His parents knew none of Carlos's friends, nor had he written about them. An average scholar, he had left school with a few O levels and had not been in any trouble. Their own investigations confirmed this.

'He was a good boy, really he was. He always made a point of mentioning Dad's football team and asking after his sisters.' Mrs Carlos dried her eyes again and Ian wondered who she was trying to convince.

At five fifteen the officers on the case were assembled in the general office. There was a feeling of imminent chaos but it was far preferable to the previous hiatus. Ian had just come back from seeing Mike Thorne and they had both agreed that, because of the lack of other instances, Carlos's death was unlikely to be a case of victimisation.

'Queer-bashing, they used to call it,' Ian had commented. 'You don't hear that expression any more.'

'Quite.' Mike Thorne's tone was disapproving. 'There haven't been any reports of violence amongst the gay community and I don't believe this is a random attack. Because the body was moved after death I'm inclined to think it more likely to be a crime of passion or a planned revenge murder. Do the usual, Ian, find out all you can about his associates.'

'Everyone,' Ian concluded. 'Every person that drinks in the Elephant, I want them all seen again.' It had to stem from there because Carlos had no family in Rickenham Green, nor was he employed. 'And I want Martin Cook brought in again.'

'Sir? The Patti Evans thing.'

'Patti Evans?'

'The woman Bruce Selby –'

'Ah, yes. A waste of time, I expect.'

78

'It was.'

But Brenda would have to type it up and file it. Later, when she had slept on it, an interesting thought occurred to her.

Leon Dawson lived in two rooms in a converted house and shared a bathroom on the landing. His needs were basic, he was not interested in material possessions, he did not smoke and he drank little. His relationships were few and far between and when they occurred they were brutal and short-lived because he was terrified of commitment and he was mentally torn by what he was. Knowing it was so yet wishing it was not, he was unable to come to terms with the inevitability that he could not change. He wished he could be more like Nigel Pollock, sure of himself, successful and with a family. Instead he had to be content to work for him; labouring, driving, anything, because he paid well and Leon enjoyed the kudos of being the one he turned to to execute the boring jobs no one else wanted. He was, he supposed, happy enough to bask in the reflected glory. Pollock was almost a hero to him.

Saturday night. Leon used the bathroom before anyone else wanted it; he changed into black jeans and a clean shirt, and splashed on some aftershave.

The streets were busy and there were people waiting for the early performance at the cinema. Where the pavement narrowed four youths blocked the way as they hung around eating burgers and chips. Leon shoved the one nearest him, their obscenities recorded but unanswered except by way of a hard shove to the biggest of them causing him to drop the polystyrene container. He stepped forward but something in Leon's face made him think better of doing anything about it.

Leon walked on. There wasn't anything he wouldn't do for Nigel and he had certainly sorted Chaz out that Thursday evening. Now there was this thing with Selby. Selby and Nigel were connected and Leon was going to find him.

As far as could be ascertained Charles Carlos was not close to any of the customers of the Pink Elephant. Most of them knew him but he was not generally liked and none of them seemed to know him well enough to want him dead. And then, just before he went home for the evening, DS Barry Swan ran their names through the computer and came up with a record of ABH for Leon Dawson. And Dawson had admitted he couldn't stand Carlos.

He passed this information on to the man relieving him and said goodnight. Lucy had not been at home when he telephoned to say he might be late and she had still to tell him where she had been the other evening. He began to see how some of the women he had taken out must have felt with his elusive and evasive answers.

He waved to Brenda Gibbons and Markham who were off on investigations of their own and drove back to his flat, relieved to find Lucy at home. He smiled at the hint of shampoo in the hall and the stronger scent of his favourite perfume. Lucy must have been in the shower and not heard the telephone.

The flat was inherited from his grandmother. Although there were windows at both ends of the long lounge, neither view was particularly inspiring. The front looked out over the parking area and two other privately owned blocks of flats across the street. Trees, still in full leaf, softened the vista.

From the back they could see into the yard of a busy body shop where, in winter, sparks from the welding equipment sprayed from open workshops like hand-held fireworks. Next to this was a depot for a sausage and pie manufacturing company where lorries arrived and departed at all hours of the day and night. Aesthetically ugly, it was, nonetheless, a view they both enjoyed because there was always something going on.

The old-fashioned furniture came with the flat but Barry had resisted the temptation to replace it because it suited the place, giving it the atmosphere of what he imagined an apartment in

Paris to possess. There was a wood-block floor and an unused fireplace with a marble surround. Both kitchen and bathroom were small but they had been subjected to modernisation.

'I hope you're hungry.' Lucy flicked back her hair, which she had taken to wearing longer lately because she said she could do more with it.

'I am.' Barry noticed that the dining-table in the back window was nicely laid and that there were wineglasses. His wife, however, was casually dressed in cotton slacks and a blouse so he had not forgotten an important date. Still, she was unpredictable, cooking an extravagant meal for no reason or suddenly announcing she had no intention of setting foot in the kitchen and it was up to Barry to do so or buy them a takeaway.

Home-made carrot and orange soup was followed by poached salmon and steamed vegetables then fruit salad. 'All very healthy,' Barry remarked when Lucy pointed out she had had all day to prepare things. Her job in the bank entailed her working some Saturdays. This week she had Friday and Saturday off but Barry had had to work.

'Yes. For good reason.'

'You're not on a diet?' There wasn't much of her now.

'Not exactly. Barry . . .' She paused, chewing her lip. 'The thing is, well, how do you feel, oh, I don't know how to put this, it wasn't at all how I rehearsed it. I'm pregnant.'

His spoon clattered into the remains of his fruit salad, the noise seeming to echo in the complete silence. 'My God!' He stared at her with his mouth open. 'My God!' he repeated before jumping up and kissing her, still unable to take it in. They had not planned to have a child for another year or so.

'You don't mind? I thought you might be angry.'

'I'm thrilled.' And he realised that he was, that he was not just saying it to make her feel better. It also explained where she had been the other evening. They would need to move, the flat had only one bedroom, but more than that, they would need to change, to adapt from their rather selfish lifestyle if they were to accommodate a baby. And there would be less money unless

Lucy went back to work. His mind was racing ahead. 'More wine. I'll open another bottle. No, not for you. Hell, I need it.' He pulled the cork from the bottle nearest to hand, not caring what it was, then picked up the telephone receiver.

'No,' Lucy said, 'not just yet. I need time to get used to it myself. And I wanted you to be the first to know.'

That evening Barry did not once think about work and his thoughts fluctuated between what he would be giving up and what he had to gain.

'What's brought this on?' Brenda said when Markham asked her to join him for a drink.

'Don't think it's your pretty little face, dear, it's work.'

'I should've guessed. And no doubt I can also guess where we're going.'

She was right. In a few minutes they entered the door of the Pink Elephant. It was busy, as Sebastian had said it would be when there was live music. 'And I can also guess why me.'

'Why?'

'Because your masculine ego would not allow you to come here off duty without a female in tow.'

'Suit yourself. What do you want to drink?'

Brenda realised she was wrong. Markham did not give a damn what anyone thought but there had to be a reason. He returned bearing a pint of lager and a Campari and soda, but he had been a long time in getting it because he had been chatting to Sebastian Roberts.

'He's remembered something else. There were a couple of blokes looking for Carlos the other night. Not local. He's given me their number.'

'Someone from the past come to find him and get even?'

'Could be. But why draw attention to yourself? Unless it's the old double bluff. They're leaving tomorrow. I'd better ring in.' Markham did so, asking for an address to be matched to the number and for someone to speak to the two men. He used the telephone on the bar but no one took any notice as what he was saying could not be heard over the music.

'Who's that?' Brenda said, nodding in the direction of a smartly dressed couple in the corner. 'Doesn't seem their sort of hang-out.'

As she spoke the man greeted Sebastian with familiarity and appeared to be introducing the woman with him. 'I've seen him before. The first time I was in here. He's not someone we've interviewed. Back in a minute.'

Once more he drew Sebastian to one side. Brenda saw him shake his head with a shocked expression on his face.

'The name's Pollock,' Markham told her, '*the* Pollock. That's the wife. He uses the place now and again, it's the first time she's been in. And guess what, Roberts thinks it's possible he was here the night both Carlos and Selby disappeared. He says, if it was the same night, he came in with another bloke, well-spoken, middle-aged.'

'Selby?'

Markham shrugged. 'Could've been. But someone like Pollock probably has many acquaintances who'd fit that description.'

'Closet queer?'

'Really, my dear,' Markham feigned shocked surprise, 'that's no way for a lady to talk.'

'Bugger off, Markham, you know what I mean.'

'Only one way to find out. If he's a regular, he must've been aware of the existence of Carlos. But not tonight, though, can't afford to be treading on the toes of local dignitaries in a public place.'

'What're we doing here?'

'I wanted to talk to you. This Railway Terrace thing, the attacks on Mrs Mostyn, don't you think it's coincidental that they've stopped since the murder, and that there've been no more outbreaks of arson?'

'Well, well. This might tie in with something I discovered today.' But she refused, for the moment, to say what. Markham raised an eyebrow and waited. 'Pollock's a builder, isn't he.' It wasn't a question, Brenda already knew.

'I'd say a bit more than a builder. It's a big company, large contracts.'

'Right. Well, supposing he wanted Railway Terrace for –'

'Already checked. He was in the middle of negotiations with a superstore who were interested in the site but they couldn't get planning permission. They didn't even bother to appeal because the technicalities of access couldn't be got around.'

'But supposing he wants it for something else?'

'Likewise. No one's been interested in that site for over a year.'

'There's something I need to know, but it'll have to wait. I promised Patti Evans something.'

'Selby's ex?'

'Yes. You see, her bungalow was built by Pollock's company.'

Markham sat back and took a long gulp of his drink. Pollock had at one time, possibly still had, an interest in Railway Terrace. Pollock was a customer of the Pink Elephant where Charles Carlos used to drink. Pollock had a connection with Bruce Selby and his ex-girlfriend who happened to be a married woman. Now, if that wasn't a nice little chain of coincidences . . . And wouldn't the Chief be interested when they told him. But, as Brenda said, it would have to wait until tomorrow, until the powers that be decided what line to take. It could even be that Martin Cook or Leon Dawson had added a bit more to their original statements and nothing further would need to be done. But Markham did not think so.

'Fancy something to eat?'

'What?' Brenda stared at him. He never socialised, she had been expecting no more than a gruff goodnight whenever they had discussed whatever it was he had brought her here for.

'Just a suggestion.'

'Well, yes, I'm hungry, actually.'

'Where?'

'Doesn't matter. Wherever we can get in.'

'Pizza then. The one in Deben Road's quite good.' It was part of Markham's staple diet because he usually got a container of salad there to take home to eat with it thus ensuring he got a few vitamins now and then.

It was already dark and the street lights cast an eerie glow over the rows of parked cars. 'Slow down,' she admonished, hurrying to keep up with his long strides. They got a table and decided to have a medium pizza each with different toppings then share them; they also ordered salad and a carafe of house white. The waitress gave them bowls for the salad.

'It's a con,' Markham said, 'you can never get enough in these.'

'Watch me.' Brenda put all the tasty bits in first then draped some lettuce over the top knowing how much room it took up in the bottom.

'No tomatoes?' They were whole and would have taken up even more space.

'Yes. Easy.' She slipped two into the pocket of her linen jacket because she needed both hands to steady the bowl. Markham grinned and followed suit, wondering if she had had enough to eat as a child. For such a slender woman she could certainly eat now.

'Has it occurred to you that either Selby or Pollock might have had a relationship with Carlos? Or even both of them.'

'Or each other,' Markham added as he poured the wine which had been placed unceremoniously on the table.

'They've got to be connected somehow.'

'Oh, they're that all right. Don't forget Selby's on the local council and where else do you go for planning permission?'

'I know, and – no, forget it.' Brenda recognised the fact that she found it difficult to switch off. 'Here's the pizza.' They shared it meticulously, cutting the threads of melted cheese, both finishing the meal at the same time because they were hungry.

'No one waiting for you?'

'It's unlike you to be so coy, Markham.' She would have expected a much saltier turn of phrase to find out if she lived alone. 'But no, there isn't. Not any more.' She was not quite ready to discuss the past and her disastrous marriage so she turned the tables. 'Why? Fancy your chances, did you? A spot of food and a

85

bottle of leg-opener back at your place. That what you had in mind?'

He laughed loudly, catching her off guard and causing other diners to turn around. It was a sound rarely heard. 'You're not serious, are you?'

'Aren't I?' Not knowing what went on in Markham's head, she was flustered and vaguely insulted. Not that she fancied him. It was rumoured that he did not have a personal life but was he actually saying he found her unattractive?

'I simply asked because we've still got some wine to finish and I didn't know if you wanted sweet and coffee. Didn't want to spoil some other man's Friday night, that's all.'

Partially mollified she declined both. 'There isn't anyone. What about you?'

'Likewise.'

A tense silence followed. It was not good policy to socialise singly with the opposite sex because of the misunderstandings that could arise at work. Brenda decided to put him straight. 'I was married. Briefly. It was a disaster and I've no intention of getting involved again. At least, not for a long time.'

Markham noted the amendment but, true to form, volunteered no information regarding himself. 'You'll get over it. Besides, you're self-reliant. It shows.'

They were hardly sympathetic words but were nevertheless true. Brenda was strong. When Harry's womanising had become too blatant to bear she had thrown him out and started to rebuild her life. By the time the decree absolute came through she felt she was ready to cope with anything. It was at that time she had applied for a transfer and finally the Rickenham Green vacancy came up. She was immediately offered the post because they were short on their quota of females in the CID.

'I'll do it,' Markham insisted when the bill arrived. 'It was my idea.' He grinned. 'And I earn more than you.'

'Only temporarily,' Brenda retaliated. She might not be able to keep up with Markham on foot but professionally she was destined to overtake him. She suspected he knew it too. When they parted she was rewarded with the gruff goodnight she had expected earlier in the evening and she was left to make her own way home.

Carol Barnes had quite enjoyed listening to local radio and did not bother to retune to Radio 4.

The following evening was cooler, too cool to take her pre-dinner drink outside. She listened to the end of a programme and waited for the news. Someone had come forward in response to the appeal because it was made clear that the body had now been positively identified.

She finally admitted that something was wrong, very wrong, and that it was time to amend the situation. She tried to fix an understanding expression on her face as she ran through ways in which she could approach the subject. There wasn't any easy solution. She opted for a direct question. But before she had enough courage to ask it she sipped a glass of rosé and unfolded the *Rickenham Herald* which she had picked up on her way home from work yesterday. As it was a weekly paper there were only three lines in the stop-press section referring to the identification for the news had come too late for proper inclusion. But there, on the bottom half of the front page, was the name Bruce Selby. Carol swallowed hard. It was seemingly unconnected with the murder yet phrased in such a way for any sensible person to make the connection.

Bruce? she thought. Surely not. She put her head in her hands and cried. Had it not been what she had suspected all along?

'Did you know him?' Anne-Marie had not missed the jerk of her husband's head when the newscaster revealed the name of the murdered man.

'Of him. He used to drink in the Elephant.'

Anne-Marie knew Nigel's firm was responsible for the rebuilding and extension and refurbishment of the pub, and he had never lied to her. She was also aware that he was involved with Bruce Selby and that he was missing. She did not want to think too closely about the implications of any of this. 'Give me a hand to put the boys to bed, would you? I don't know what's got into them today.'

Glad of the distraction, Nigel followed her upstairs to the playroom. He bathed both his sons in the same water whilst Anne-Marie got out clean nightclothes. He handed her the younger, wrapped in a towel, then applied soap to the older boy. Chaz was not a pleasant character but who on earth would want to kill him? As he rinsed off the soap one name came to mind. The question was, what was he going to do about it?

'Our friend Lara is coming too,' Moira informed Ian when he arrived home that evening.

'That'll be fun.'

'Yes, well, I need you to get the bed down from the loft at some point. I'll clear out the spare room tomorrow. I take it you're going in?'

'I have to.'

'I know. I wasn't criticising.'

'When are they coming?'

'Tuesday.'

'Do you suppose she's learned how to talk yet?'

'She'll be all right, she's probably just shy. Anyway, it's company for Mark, we'll be at work all day.'

'Hasn't he got any other friends round here?'

'Ian, leave it. You know what he's like, he's as stubborn as you are. If we make any objections he'll dig his heels in and if we don't make her welcome he won't bother coming home again.'

Ian resented being called stubborn but was honest enough not to argue with the truth. 'Meanwhile, where's all that junk going?'

'Either in the loft or in the dustbin. Most of it's yours.'

'Well, give it to Deirdre for one of her endless jumble sales.'

Moira had been right about Mark wanting to bring Lara with

him but she had stipulated the conditions. 'Lara goes in the spare bedroom and no musical beds in the night or your father'll go mad,' she told him. Mark had been shocked at her direct approach but Moira knew there would be opportunity enough during the day if their relationship had reached that stage.

With some food inside him Ian felt more human and, to make amends for his earlier abruptness, promised they would have a day out, by themselves, next weekend, work permitting.

Light was barely filtering through the curtains when the alarm went off and Ian wondered if he had set it wrongly. Only when the wraithlike strands of his dream slipped away, one in which football rather than victims and suspects was prominent, did he realise that what he could hear was rain and not the roar of the crowd and that the darkness was due to the low, grey sky rather than floodlight failure at a crucial moment when he was about to score the winning goal for Norwich. This was no heavy shower but a constant pattering against the window, the sort of rain that was here to stay.

The traffic which always increased in such conditions was slowly building up when he left Belmont Terrace. There would be a few people, like himself, who would be going to work, but most of the cars contained couples or families going to spend the day with friends or relations or doing whatever normal people did on Saturdays. Soggy litter from Friday night's gastronomical delights lay in the gutters depressingly; chip papers and takeaway cartons. Undiscerning pigeons and starlings picked at the left-overs. Things had changed since Ian's day, when all they had to look forward to at the weekend was the youth club.

He had to brake suddenly when an elderly woman, hidden beneath a golfing umbrella, stepped out into the road without looking and reached the opposite side without being aware she had been in any danger. Deaf maybe? Whatever, Ian hoped she was not about to become another statistic. He was edgy and irritable but with what or whom he did not know. 'What a God-awful world this is,' he muttered, noticing the bottles lined up on the pavement outside the Feathers. He knew the landlord, who must be unaware of what was going on because he ran a tight ship. Ian was surprised he had fallen for the trick of a legal drinker buying a round and passing drinks to his under-age friends in the street. Still, if it was very busy it might not be obvious.

'What've I missed?' DS Barry Swan was looking unusually smug.

'Nothing. Why?'

'What're you so bloody cheerful about then?'

'It's the rain. I just love wet weather.'

Ian sighed. No point in continuing if Barry was in one of his frivolous moods. 'Who else is in?'

'Markham and Gibbons.'

They were missing DC Alan Campbell who, with his fixation for computers and his unquestioned ability in correlating evidence, was away on a course. No replacement had been offered either.

'Go and see him,' Ian said when he heard what Markham and DC Gibbons had come up with.

'I need to make a phone call first, sir.' Brenda dialled Patti Evans's number, apologised for bothering her again and asked one question.

She turned around with an expression of satisfaction. 'Mr and Mrs Evans', she said, 'used to live in Railway Terrace.'

'In that case, I think I'll visit Pollock myself. Get me the statements taken last night first.'

Leon Dawson and Martin Cook had each spent several hours being reinterviewed. Cook, Ian saw, had provided a rota of his duties during the relevant period; there were still times not accounted for, but there was no reason for holding him although he had a possible motive. Leon Dawson was not so easy to deal with. He had objected to being questioned a second time, demanded a solicitor and remained sullen and uncooperative throughout the interview. There was no mention of Nigel Pollock, but at the time it was not known that he used the same pub.

'I told you before', he had said, 'that I didn't like Chaz. Lots of people didn't like him, doesn't mean I killed him.' But he had refused to say why he did not like him. 'So?' he had answered in response to the fact that he had been seen leaving the Pink Elephant at roughly the same time as Chaz and that saying he had gone straight home, alone, was not much of an alibi.

'Look, I didn't know I'd need one. Have you finished?' The duty solicitor had interrupted once or twice, but only to warn Leon it was best not to lose his temper.

'You have a bit of a temper, don't you, Mr Dawson?' DC Brown had asked. 'And it's got you in trouble before.' Brown hated working at night and he did not like the person he was interviewing. It showed, much as he tried to disguise it, and Leon knew it.

'You didn't need to ask me that. If you're as efficient as you make out you'll have every last detail on that little incident. It still doesn't mean I killed Chaz. I'm not going to answer any more questions so can I go?' And that was the end of the interview.

'Who're these people?' Ian put down the copies he had read and stared at the names Phillip James Harman and Dennis Watson.

'Old friends of the victim, so they say.' It was Markham who answered. 'Roberts told me last night they'd called in looking for him. Left a contact number behind the bar for Carlos to ring.' The late shift had been more efficient than Dawson gave them credit for. They had traced the address and brought the two men in.

It had, Ian realised, been a hectic night and suddenly they were surrounded by suspects but still none the wiser as to Selby's part, if any, in all of it.

'Brenda, I'd like you to check out their backgrounds and find out their real reason for being in Rickenham. It's hardly a holiday resort. See what their connection was with Carlos in Bristol. I'm going to see Pollock.'

'There's one more thing,' Markham said as Ian was leaving, 'probably not relevant, but there's been no more vandalism in Railway Terrace since the murder.'

'No, and that brings us back to Pollock again.'

'And the arson attacks, do you suppose they were a diversion?'

'It might well be. We haven't yet got the bugger, but at least it's stopped.'

Ian was wrong. There had been another one the previous night which, because of the importance of the case they were working on, had not yet filtered through to them.

PC Mallet, back from his days off, felt the water trickle down the neck of his waterproof which he had not been expecting to wear for several weeks yet. The thunderstorm two days ago had cleared the air but only enough to allow a band of low pressure to move in. However, for a man who spent so much of his time out of doors, weather was of little consequence to PC Mallet, who only noticed it when it was extreme.

On familiar territory, he strolled in the direction of the disused railway tracks. They were divided from the pavement by a mesh-link fence through which rank-smelling weeds straggled, battered down by the rain. Signs proclaimed that the area was patrolled by security men and dogs. He had yet to see either. The only time anyone had been on the other side of the fence was when two boys had athletically clambered over it. He had turned a blind eye. There was nothing there which needed protection and nothing to harm the boys. There was certainly no danger from trains.

His sergeant had told him all was quiet and he was pleased. As if his thoughts had conjured her up he saw Mrs Mostyn in a fawn raincoat and a plastic rain hood hurrying towards the corner shop. He called out a greeting but she did not turn around because she was partially deaf in one ear and the rain on the hood obliterated other sounds.

Mr Gilbert was staring disconsolately out of his window but his face lit up when he saw his friend. His house, opposite Mrs Mostyn's, was in far better condition because he had had more money. Or so he thought. At least the house was paid for before the news broke about Maxwell and he was left with only his state pension. No real friendship had formed between him and Mrs Mostyn, despite PC Mallet's encouragement. Later he realised the two neighbours had had their lives and did not want to make new attachments, having lost too much already, and that some days it was enough just to keep going.

Mr Gilbert tapped on the window when the tall figure was near enough to hear and the door was open before PC Mallet had time to cross the road.

'It's too damn dark to paint today and electric's no good for my eyes these days. I've got nothing new to show you but I dare say you wouldn't say no to a coffee. You must be cold and wet,' he finished persuasively.

'Coffee?'

'Yes. Come out here and see.' In the modern conversion of the kitchen Mr Gilbert proudly displayed a hamper of basic groceries he had won as third prize in a raffle at the British Legion. He unscrewed the jar of Nescafé and removed the foil with a faint but permanent tremor. PC Mallet marvelled at how such hands could perform such intricate detail in the water-colours. 'First time I've ever won anything,' he continued. 'And all this for 10p.'

PC Mallet was touched. The draw, he knew, was on Thursday nights but Mr Gilbert had waited to share his little bit of luck with him.

'Do you think it's stopped for good?'

'It hasn't.'

'Not the rain, you daft bugger.' Mr Gilbert chuckled. 'Mrs Mostyn's troubles. I saw her yesterday and there's been nothing else since she got back from visiting her daughter. Down to you, is it? Like those crime busters on TV?' His tone was gently teasing. 'Anyway, I've been keeping a look-out like you said but I sleep at the back since Elsie died. I just can't think who'd want to upset a nice old dear like that.'

'Well, if you do see anything, you know where to find me. We appreciate your help, you know.' Mr Gilbert had not actually given any help but it made him feel more part of things and gave him something to do. 'I'd better be on my way.'

'That's it, son. Out on the streets, fighting crime. Here, just a minute.' They were standing in the doorway, PC Mallet on the front step. 'There was someone knocked on her door when she was away. Youngish chap. I'd completely forgotten it until now. That's what reminded me.' He nodded in the direction of her house. A postman who finished his round in Railway Terrace was knocking on her door. 'She's down the shop,' Mr Gilbert called. 'Tell him, will you? He can't hear me.' But Mrs Mostyn was on her way back up the street before PC Mallet could oblige.

'I don't suppose you can remember what he looked like?'

'Only saw him for a minute or so. Middling's the word that comes to mind. Brownish hair, medium-sized – no, my memory's not what it was. He had a leather jacket on though, I remember that much. Daft, I thought, because it was so warm.'

PC Mallet put his notebook away. Mr Gilbert was confused. Markham had called in to see Mrs Mostyn and Markham was never without his leather jacket.

'Is that helpful?'

'Extremely.'

'I'll be getting a name for myself, what's it they call them? Snout?' Mr Gilbert chuckled again, pleased with his technical knowledge.

PC Mallet replaced his helmet and went out into the dismal street. Had he not started to make a note of what he had been told he would have forgotten all about the man in the leather jacket.

DCI Roper had to admit he was impressed when he saw where Pollock lived. Still, if a man who owned companies of those dimensions could not provide himself with a decent place to live, then no one could. Unlike other buildings erected by the nouveau riche this one was tasteful; not at all the Sunday supplement stuff with gables and dormer windows and paved-over front gardens to accommodate several luxury cars. Not a mock carriage lamp in sight, no Georgian columns or statuary bought at the local garden centre and no mullioned windows. In fact none of the things Ian disliked, which predisposed him to like the man himself. Instead he faced a pleasing, rectangular building of local stone; the windows might be double glazed but they were of the sash variety, in keeping with the proportions, and the front door was plain wood with an old-fashioned knocker, an original by the rust on it. There was a garage but it was set discreetly to the right of and slightly back from the house and the garden was pretty without being over-neat.

'Good morning, can I help you?' A thickset man in a short dressing-gown opened the door. In his hand was a mug of something and there was a newspaper under his arm.

'Chief Inspector Roper. May I come in?'

Pollock glanced briefly at the identification and nodded. 'Yes, of course. Forgive me.' He looked at the sky and shook his head. 'That's our weekend plans ruined.'

The lounge reaffirmed Ian's first impressions. The suite was covered in a pale blue velvety material but looked comfortable, and although some of the pieces of furniture were possibly antiques there were scratches and marks of wear and tear. There were books and magazines and children's toys. It was a large version of his own home and he realised immediately that was why he felt so comfortable as soon as he was shown in. Not the toys, though, not any more, not unless or until Mark produced grandchildren. He pushed the thought of Lara being the mother of those children to the back of his mind.

'What is it you want to see me about, Chief Inspector?'

Urbane was the word which sprang to Ian's mind. Polite, welcoming and remembering his rank. He would ask if he wanted coffee next. Pollock did so. Ian declined, then thought better of it.

'Are you sure? My wife'll fetch you some.'

'If it's no bother.' It was a way of getting an impression of the wife without asking to see her. If she was pushy, demanding and

96

avaricious it might suggest a reason for Pollock being involved. If he was involved.

'Anne-Marie?' Pollock briefly left the room. As the door opened Ian heard the sound of children's voices. 'Now, let's hear it.'

'You can't have failed to have heard about the death of Charles Carlos . . .'

'Ah, of course, I should've guessed. You're here because I occasionally use the Pink Elephant and that's where he mostly did his drinking. I only heard last night that he'd been identified, I'd no idea. I suppose you want to know if I knew Chaz? Yes, I did, as far as anyone ever knows a fellow drinker. It's all right, sweetheart, you can come in.'

Anne-Marie had knocked on the door, a strange action, Ian thought, in one's own home. 'I'll be right back,' she said, smiling at her visitor. Firm instructions to the children were issued from the bottom of the stairs. 'Or you won't go to the swimming pool this afternoon,' were the final words.

More plus points, Ian thought. Parents who did not mind their children playing in their lounge and who obviously believed in bringing them up with some discipline, and no swimming pool of their own. Anne-Marie returned and poured the coffee, first asking if they wanted her to stay.

'Of course. The Chief Inspector needs to ask some questions about that murder.'

Anne-Marie sat in one of the armchairs, her body language conveying that she was not totally relaxed. Was Ian's presence alone responsible or was there more to it?

'I was saying I use the pub, ridiculous name, but there you are. I know Sebastian Roberts well – keeps his beer in excellent condition, by the way, and none of those awful machines. I know what sort of establishment it is but that sort of thing doesn't bother me. Besides, the lad's done well for himself, attracted a mixed clientele and got most of the Town Hall trade too, I believe.'

Ian nodded in encouragement. Was Pollock talking too much or was he simply used to holding the floor?

'Chaz spoke to me a couple of times, no chat-up, nothing like that, but for some reason I took an instant dislike to him, don't ask me why.' Pollock shrugged and held his hands palms uppermost. They were large hands, strong enough to kill someone of Carlos's size easily, except he was rich enough to pay someone to do it for him. Anne-Marie, an attractive natural blonde with an unmade-up face, was watching her husband.

'Since you arrived I've been trying to figure out when I last saw Chaz. It was a week ago last Thursday.'

'You seem certain. For someone who doesn't know him well.'

'I'm certain all right. You see, I know it was Thursday because I was there with Bruce Selby and it was his council meeting night and he had to leave early. I think it was too noisy for him anyway, there was some sort of birthday bash going on and it was very crowded. And Bruce has gone AWOL as well. I really don't know what's going on but one thing I'm certain of, Sebastian's got nothing to do with it. He's straight as a die, that one.' Pollock, hands now in his dressing-gown pockets, grinned. 'Well, you know what I mean.'

'What's your connection with Selby?'

'He's on the planning committee. I thought everyone knew that. It's a good connection to have, helps oil the wheels, as they say.'

'What time did Selby leave?'

'Oh, I couldn't say. He refused another drink when I offered, but I left before he did.'

'At what time?'

'Am I under suspicion, Chief Inspector?'

'I just need to verify the facts.' Ian knew he sounded pompous but he did not want to give anything away.

'I can't remember exactly. Ah, you could try the taxi firm I use. They picked me up, I never drink and drive, you see, because I was meeting my wife at the Elms.'

Naturally someone like Pollock would belong to the Elms Golf and Country Club. Joining fees were prohibitive yet the waiting list was not short. Its advantage was that one of the restaurants was open to the general public and was widely used by those celebrating special occasions or for wedding receptions. It must be raking in a fortune. Doc Harris was a member but he reckoned the membership was worth it for what he saved on the cheap doubles they sold.

'I had the car,' Anne-Marie volunteered. 'I'm not bothered about drinking. The table was booked for eight thirty but Nigel got there before that because we went to the bar.'

And the Elms was a good fifteen-minute drive from the Pink Elephant, which meant he probably left at around seven thirty. In which case what was Selby still doing in the pub when he should have been at his meeting, unless he never intended going to it?

'How often did you see Mr Selby?'

'I'm confused. I thought it was Chaz you wanted to know about.'

'I do. But hasn't it struck you as odd that that was the last time both of them were seen?'

'Good God, you can't think old Bruce had anything to do with it? You don't know the man, he's incapable of violence. Once or twice a month is the answer to your question.'

'All right. Now what about Gareth Evans?'

Pollock, stunned, sat down but it did not diminish his powerful presence. He shook his head in bewilderment. 'I'm not sure you've told me exactly what all this is about, but I've nothing to hide. Gareth Evans is crippled. I bought their house and built them a custom-built bungalow. They did extremely well out of the deal, as did I. The agreement was that I could use the bungalow, with them *in situ*, for a year as a show-piece. I know what you must think of me, that it was taking advantage of a couple in a vulnerable position who probably needed time to adjust to their new circumstances, but they gained financially and physically. They could not have stayed where they were and they could not have afforded what I provided – and although my reasons for the offer were far from altruistic, I can't help feeling that having people look around the place for those first twelve months probably helped take their minds off the problem.'

'And what did you gain out of it, Mr Pollock?'

'I gained a big fat contract to erect the neurological hospital at Saxborough and several other similar bungalows. And before you mention it, yes, it was Bruce who inspected the bungalow and there were no strings pulled either. He's good, but I'm bloody good. Just ask anyone I've done work for.' Pollock was becoming angry, for no real reason Ian could see. But he did have a point, his reputation as a builder was excellent.

'My husband has hardly ever had a complaint, the few he has had have been the fault of workmen and they're asked to leave. Nigel makes sure the matter's put right immediately, at no extra cost.'

The loyal little wife, Ian thought. Anne-Marie did not come across as any of the things he had expected, neither did she seem to have much going for her in the way of personality, but the couple were close, he could tell that, and for all his posturing, he still could not bring himself to dislike Nigel Pollock.

Ian thanked them both for their time and returned to the station. In his office, coffee at hand, he drew a diagram.

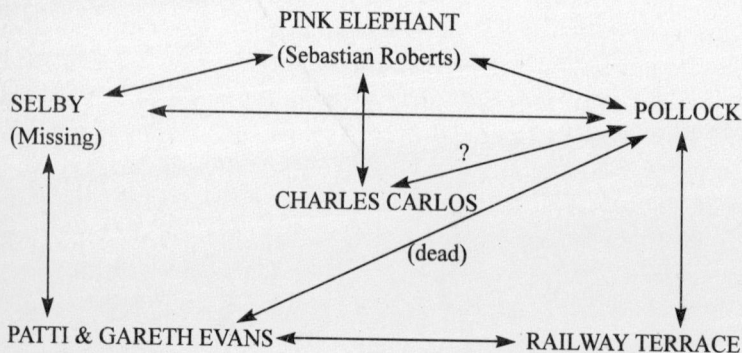

```
                    PINK ELEPHANT
                   (Sebastian Roberts)
  SELBY                                          POLLOCK
 (Missing)                          ?
                    CHARLES CARLOS

                        (dead)

PATTI & GARETH EVANS              RAILWAY TERRACE
```

So what did it mean? Yes, the connections were all there but if Pollock was to be believed, which Ian thought he might be, it was all on a business level. Still, he had left asking the man about his interest in Railway Terrace for a future time. He had been confident and assured, he might not be with a second visit. His pen hovered over the name Gareth Evans. It might be worth finding out exactly what sort of accident it was.

He took one last glance at his drawing. Without question Pollock was the link.

Brenda Gibbons, having warned Patti Evans that she was coming, walked across the reception area and saw Markham appearing from the direction of the general office. 'Morning,' she said. He did not reply. 'Have I done something to offend you?' Her voice was loud enough for the desk sergeant to hear, which was intended. Others might accept his rudeness, she would not.

'What?' He stared at her. 'Sorry, I was thinking. What did you say?'

'Forget it.' She pushed her way angrily through the revolving doors, perfectly sure he had heard her the first time.

Brenda overlapped the edges of her raincoat and held it tightly against her as she hurried to the front door of the bungalow. Shrubs and trees dripped but their leaves shone, laurels and bay glossy, the roses refreshed. Through the plate glass window she saw the outline of a wheelchair. Gareth Evans was home, she would have to tread carefully. She rang the bell in case she had not been seen and heard the swish of rubber on tiles. Expertly, and with plenty of room in which to do so, he opened the door with its waist-height handle and smiled pleasantly. Evans, she decided, was an extremely handsome man. What had such a fate done to him mentally? His hair was thick and fair and his torso well muscled: it must be hell to be confined to that chair.

'Come in. My wife's expecting you.'

Drops of water clung to her hair and dampened the shoulders of her mac. There was nowhere to wipe her feet, presumably because a mat would hinder the chair. 'It's all right,' Evans said, realising what she was looking for. 'That's why it's tiled. You can't wipe wheels.'

'Mr Evans, I spoke to your wife recently, I expect she told you.'
Brenda was indeed playing it carefully.

'She did. Something about this murder.'

Interesting. Brenda could not recall mentioning that, she had only come about Bruce Selby. Was it guesswork after having read the *Rickenham Herald*, protection, because she did not want her husband to guess what had really happened, or did Patti Evans know more than she was saying? 'Yes. I know it must have been a difficult time for you, but can you recall anything about the man who built this house, or the surveyor?'

'Are they involved?'

'We don't know.'

'Not really. Not even their names. As you say, it was a rather difficult time.' He stressed the last but one word cynically. 'It was a long time ago, we never saw them after that first year.'

'Hello.' Patti Evans stood in the doorway. She might have been there some time waiting to see if Brenda kept to her word. 'Anyone want coffee?'

Gareth shook his head and Brenda said she would not be staying long, then, deciding there was no easy way around the question, asked outright: 'How did the accident happen, Mr Evans?'

When he scowled his face altered, showing the lines etched by pain and frustration. He laughed bitterly. 'It was what they call an industrial accident and of all life's ironies, it has to be the best. I worked for a large insurance company. A container lorry lost control on a hill over near Saxborough, and how many hills are there in this county? It ploughed into the side of a house. It was supposed to have been rendered safe and I was assessing the damage.' He stopped, remembering that day, and Brenda wished she had not had to ask. 'I tripped and crashed into the unstable wall. It collapsed bringing down a joist which landed across my back. I was wearing the mandatory headgear. It saved my life.' His tone was bitter. 'I wish I hadn't been.' There was no self-pity, it was a statement of fact. 'Well, you can see we've ended up better off than some in our position. We've got this

102

place and the personal injury pay-off and my pension. Would you excuse me?' He turned the chair abruptly and wheeled himself from the room.

'I'm sorry,' Brenda said as Patti stood up. 'It needed to be asked. I wouldn't have done it otherwise.'

'You really thought someone had harmed Gareth deliberately?'

'It was a possibility.'

'Well, you were wrong. Is there anything else?'

'No. I really am sorry.' She suspected that Patti Evans would not have an easy day ahead of her now.

She had, however, eliminated the possibility that Pollock, or someone working for him, had engineered the accident.

The continous rain did nothing to alleviate the vague depression which was settling upon her. Patti Evans loved her husband and, injured though he was, would stick it out. She, Brenda Jane Gibbons, had managed to lose her husband to another woman in the space of two years.

Carol Barnes had not slept and it showed. Her hair, loose around her face, was unflattering and the skin beneath her eyes was puffy. She had shed more than a few tears once her questions had been answered and now, in the grey light of a wet morning, she had her own position to consider. She filled the kettle, her bare feet cold on the flagstone floor.

I've been such a fool, she thought as fresh tears filled her eyes. She wiped them away impatiently with the sleeve of her dressing-gown. Right from the start she had had her doubts. From experience she ought to have known it was too good to last. It was always the same, she had been attracted for the wrong reasons. Weakness was weakness whichever way you looked at it, but she had allowed herself to believe that it could be overcome; alone or with the aid of someone strong like herself.

Carol sniffed and blew her nose. I'm intelligent and professional, she thought. I won't let this beat me. Her general philosophy had always been that problems were there merely to be solved. There had to be a way around this one but it might take more time than she had to find it.

The blue china teapot stood on the mat on the kitchen table. It held six cups and she would probably drink them all. Tea and a couple of cigarettes were her usual breakfast. There was a no-smoking policy at work so she had to content herself at home or if she went out in the lunch hour. It was still early and although it was a dull day the sun had risen at six. She sighed. Had she taken on too much? Now she knew, it seemed the responsibility was to be all hers.

A blackbird hopped across the grass, in its element as the wet soil yielded the worms more easily. If only life were that simple, she thought, with nothing to worry about except where the next meal was coming from. She saw the absurdity of the idea. How dull it would be and even blackbirds had to suffer predators and cats and harsh winters.

There had been three longish relationships in Carol's life, and a couple of extremely short-lived ones. She had always been content with a quiet life; her evenings spent reading or listening to music. Cooking was another hobby she enjoyed, even when it was only for herself. In retrospect she knew she had always been an outsider, that parties and pubs and late nights had never appealed even when she was a teenager.

Self-deception was not something with which she could usually upbraid herself but she was aware she had succumbed to it lately; worse, she had also been guilty of putting two and two together and managing to make that wrong. Her dilemma was what her course of action was to be. She needed time but that was the one thing she did not have.

'Deirdre? Fancy coming over for a coffee?' It was only eight thirty, fifteen minutes after Ian had departed, but Moira's widowed friend was an early riser and would probably have already cleaned the house and got the washing in the machine. Deirdre had a tumble drier. Glancing out of the window Moira decided she might invest in one too. 'The thing is, you can have the pick of the stuff in the spare room if you come.'

'You'll be sorry. I know that husband of yours.'

'It was his idea.'

'In that case, what time shall I come and how many bin liners shall I bring?'

'Oh, about ten. And don't worry, I've got plenty of bags. I bought them on the last occasion we were supposed to be having a clear-out.'

'I'll see you later.' Deirdre hung up.

Moira went around with duster and vacuum cleaner and put some ground coffee on. When Deirdre arrived they went through the boxes, which seemed to have accumulated of their own accord. It was a long time since they had used the spare room; Mark's friends, when they had stayed, had been male and had slept in the second bed in his room. By noon the ten by eight space had reverted to a bedroom. She helped Deirdre lug the sacks out to the boot of the car and wondered if she had been a bit rash. Guaranteed, in a week or so she or Ian would suddenly decide they needed one of the items they had not set eyes on for months. But Deirdre slammed the lid of the boot down decisively, pecked her on the cheek and drove off with a thank you and a wave.

Taking an umbrella Moira walked the quarter of a mile into the town centre and ran into Lucy Swan who was carrying one small plastic bag adorned with the name of a lingerie shop. It contained, no doubt, some flimsy article for the titillation of Mr Swan. Lucy looked quite radiant as they exchanged a few words and, although she did not say anything, Moira wondered if she was pregnant. When they parted she went into Boots to buy a wash-in hair colour which helped maintain the blonde-ness. She had applied it and showered before Ian returned later that afternoon.

'I've done the spare room,' she told him. 'Go and have a look.'

He did so but seemed preoccupied when he said it was much better. However, considering it was a wet Saturday afternoon and he had missed one of Norwich's early season matches, she supposed he was in a reasonable frame of mind.

'What's that?' He had placed the diagram on the table after pouring a glass of Adnams from a two-litre plastic bottle.

'Just ideas.'

Moira picked up some ironing she had done and removed his damp jacket from the back of the chair. 'I'll take this too,' she said pointedly, with no effect.

'You could pour me a glass of wine,' she shouted down the stairs as she stacked the folded clothes and linen in the airing cupboard. There were times when his cavalier attitude irritated her. Although she knew he tried to be otherwise, and even though she, too, worked full time, he was still in the habit of leaving clothes for her to pick up and often took it for granted that she would wait on him, leaving empty plates or mugs or glasses wherever he happened to be sitting. If she asked him to put the kettle on it was some time before he moved and she, quicker in every respect, would end up doing it herself.

It was the niggling little pains in her abdomen which alerted her to the cause of her tetchiness, but knowing the cause did not prevent her feeling that way.

'Ian, I asked you to pour me a glass of wine.'

'I was waiting for you to come down.' He stood up and stepped across to the fridge, opened the door and stared at the contents for several seconds before he withdrew the opened bottle of white with its sealed stopper. 'This whole thing revolves around the Pink Elephant,' he said, as if the sight of alcohol had prompted the remark.

'What thing?'

'This case. The murder.' He poured the wine and handed it to Moira.

'You think the owner's responsible?'

'No.' But had Sebastian Roberts been investigated fully? Where, for instance, did he get the money to buy the pub from the brewery and then have all the alterations carried out? 'Pollock!' he said. Of course. Had he also done Roberts a favour,

106

and if so, what, and what did he want in return? He had as much as admitted nothing was for nothing in this world as far as he was concerned.

'Pardon?'

'I'm just going to make a phone call, then the evening's yours.'

Moira bit her tongue. It was useless trying to get through to him when he was thinking about work and if he carried on like this their day out tomorrow would end up being cancelled as well.

'Who is Pollock?'

'The owner of a very large concern. A builder originally but he's now got several companies under one umbrella; bathroom fittings, patio and conservatory construction, painting and decorating, anything to do with houses. He seems to be connected with everyone we've investigated so far.' He groaned. 'I'm sorry, Moira, one more call and I promise that's it. You can unplug the phone then if you want.'

When he returned to the kitchen Ian was satisfied that Sebastian Roberts's background was being investigated and inquiries were being carried out as to whether Leon Dawson also had any connection with Nigel Pollock.

'Why is it you suddenly think of these things the minute you get in the door?' She was not nagging but genuinely curious.

'Something to do with being away from the pressure maybe, different surroundings, distancing myself? I don't know. Mind, talking to you always helps.' This was true. By explaining or discussing cases with someone who was not *au fait* with the facts, his own thoughts became clarified and there had been times when Moira's own input had been more than useful. He studied Moira properly. She seemed a bit tired, but cleaning out the spare room had been strenuous – even so, in jeans and sweatshirt, dishevelled, she could still walk out of the door and find not only a man younger than himself but, he suspected, one younger than her. It was a sobering thought and he made an effort to give her his undivided attention. It was not to be. Moira

107

started asking questions about Charles Carlos and Ian answered them.

'That must be so hard to live with. For both of them.' She was referring to Patti and Gareth Evans. Moira glanced around the kitchen; neither it, nor the rest of the house, was suitable for someone wheelchair-bound. If anything happened to either of them they would have to move. The upheaval, on top of everything else, would be difficult to bear. She shivered at the thought.

On Sunday the rain was too heavy to consider doing anything special. Contemplating the imminent visit of Mark and Lara, they made the most of it and settled for a traditional roast and an afternoon with the papers. In the evening Moira insisted on a walk but Ian did not object as there was only half an hour to opening time.

Leon Dawson had never learned to cope with leisure time; given his own way he would work and eat and sleep. Occasionally he went to the cinema but was usually bored before the end of the film. On Sunday afternoon he lay on his bed, hands clasped behind his head, trying not to listen to the television blaring away next door.

In the drawer of the teak-veneered bedside cabinet was a Polaroid snapshot of Chaz with his arm around Bruce Selby's shoulders. It was taken the night they had both disappeared, by one of the crowd in the pub, Leon did not know who, and he had made it his business to retrieve it from Chaz, which had not been easy. He took it out and stared at it. Selby looked uncomfortable. Taking it to the kitchenette he lit a match from the large box next to the gas cooker, held it to one corner until the snapshot stared to curl and dropped it in the sink. It did not burn well and he had to light it again. The edges turned green and yellow and there was a strong smell of chemicals. Finally, when the men were no longer distinguishable, he threw it in the bin.

Tomorrow, Monday, he would begin his search for Bruce Selby and he had a very rough idea of where to start.

Although he was not averse to putting in an appearance at the station when he was officially off duty, Markham avoided it that Sunday because he knew Brenda Gibbons would be there. It was not her he was eschewing. For a woman, in fact, as far as anyone was concerned, she was not bad to work with. She was hard and he liked that, but he did not want her to start getting the wrong idea. They were both in the process of making their positions clear.

She was, he thought, turning out to be a very good replacement for DC Emmanuel who had joined them when he was tired of city policing and being chased by married women. Surprisingly, big and black as he was, he had fitted in. Surprisingly because although there were Asians in Rickenham Green there were few, if any, Africans. If people stared he ignored them, if he was snubbed he grinned and even Markham had to accept that grin had women on their knees in seconds. In a rare moment of intimacy Winston Emmanuel admitted he actually missed the city and he missed the women. He said he would not feel truly at ease in a mixed relationship, not because he was racist but because he was lazy and preferred to avoid the potential hazards. His loud laugh and vulgar wit had been missed but people moved around in the job and it did not do to get too close.

Once some basic tidying up was done Markham spent most of the lunchtime in the Black Horse. Now that drinking hours had been extended to all day on Sundays there was a temptation to prolong his stay but Markham knew his faults. Three drinks and he was happy to leave and do something else, if he bought the fourth there was no telling where it would end. He was not hungry because he had had a bacon sandwich for breakfast but the thought of staring at the television screen was depressing. He would walk, it would do him good. He placed his glass decisively on the bar counter and left the pub. Shoulders hunched, head down against the rain, he went up the High Street, crossed the bridge and turned down Deben Lane. An almost circular walk of the town would take up most of the afternoon. Puddles lay in the narrow road behind the Poplars Business Park and the wooden fence at the back of Bradley Court housing estate was once more broken. Kids, he thought, knowing he had done the same in his youth. Far better to pull out a few slats to squeeze through than walk through all the houses. On past the railway station, round by the derelict sidings and into Railway Terrace. The corner shop was open, taking advantage of the new laws presumably, enabling them to sell alcohol on a Sunday afternoon. When did they have a break? Still, it might pay off, there were four customers inside.

PC Mallet had passed on what Mr Bertram Gilbert had said, about seeing him call upon Mrs Mostyn, but Gilbert had claimed it was whilst she was away. Old as he was, would he be that much mistaken? Markham decided to alleviate the boredom of Mr Gilbert's Sunday afternoon.

Bert Gilbert, however, was far from bored although he was disgruntled when he opened the door. As it was too dull to paint, he had taken his few bits to the launderette, had a bottle of Mackesons at the Legion then cooked himself some liver with boiled potatoes and cabbage. Having stacked the dishes in a bowl under the sink to attend to later he had sat down to watch *The Dambusters*; he had seen it many times before but this did not detract from his enjoyment of it.

He sighed when Markham introduced himself. PC Mallet was a good bloke, nice to have a bit of a chat with, but Bert Gilbert did not want his house overrun with policemen.

Markham smiled, which always had the opposite effect from that intended. Mr Gilbert kept him on the doorstep. 'One of our men says you witnessed a man in a leather jacket knocking on Mrs Mostyn's door. Is that right?'

'It is. I do my bit, I like to give Jim Mallet a hand.'

'And this was when the lady was away?'

'Yes. Oh, I see. You think I'm making it up to keep in his good books.'

'No. But what I wanted to ask you, could it have been me you saw?'

Mr Gilbert studied the leather-jacketed figure in front of him and shook his head. 'Definitely not. His hair was lighter, and longer than yours, over the collar, and he wasn't quite so tall or broad across the shoulders.'

'This him?' Markham produced a copy of a photograph supplied by Doreen Carlos.

'Yes.' Mr Gilbert's head shot up and there was a smile in his eyes. 'Is that who's been bothering her?' He was thrilled to think he was responsible for identifying the culprit.

'Maybe. But he's also the man who was murdered recently.'

'Never.'

'Thanks very much, Mr Gilbert. We might need you to make a statement to that effect. Someone'll let you know.' Markham left without looking back.

If Bert Gilbert thought more praise was to be forthcoming he was mistaken, but he didn't know Markham. 'He's been drinking,' he muttered to himself, having smelled the beer on Markham's breath. He closed the living-room door and picked up the threads of the story.

If Pollock was behind it, had, for example, used Carlos to frighten the residents, what was the purpose behind it? The supermarket chain had pulled out and the council had not received any further applications for the area. The site, because of access difficulties, was not suitable for anything on a grand scale which ruled out a leisure centre or sports complex or even a hotel or cinema. All that left was small business premises or private residences, which would not bring in much of a return for his investment. Or would they?

DC Gibbons had accepted Barry Swan's offer of a quick drink on the way home. The new licensing laws might not be acceptable to some people but to shift workers or those who worked unsociable hours it was certainly pleasant to be able to enjoy a pint at five thirty on a Sunday afternoon.

'The Chief's always saying "Know the man and you'll know his enemies," ' Brenda commented when she had a Campari and soda in front of her. Barry had not met anyone else who drank it. 'But in this instance, no one we've interviewed seems to be able to tell us much about him.'

'A loner, probably, didn't get close to people.'

'He did. There was the boyfriend.'

But Martin Cook worked long hours and only saw Charles Carlos for short periods. Even so, considering the length of time the relationship had lasted, he still seemed to know little about him.

They remained standing at the bar because they were only having one drink. There was a steady trade and the ubiquitous Sky sports channel was on the television. 'We do know a few facts, I suppose. He was a good son, he was gay, he was having boyfriend trouble, he was a regular, but not heavy drinker, he was known to Pollock and, therefore, possibly Selby, who has now disappeared.' Brenda tossed back her hair and gained an admiring glance from a red-faced man who had probably been there some hours. To Barry's astonishment she winked at him, whereby the man suddenly found it necessary to study the list of prices fixed to the beam beside him. 'Well,' she said, 'it's supposed to be an equal world.' She knew it was not so, that a man could get away with it but coming from a female it mostly caused shock or embarrassment. It did the trick anyway and prevented men bothering her. 'There's nothing back from Forensics yet.'

'Do you think that's important?'

'Of course. Think about it, what if he was HIV positive or into drugs?'

'The post-mortem . . .'

'Yes, but none of it was conclusive. And where did he get the money he must have had to live the way he did? It didn't all

112

come from the benefits office. Do you want another one? Good, because I'm off now. Things to do.' Brenda said goodbye to the landlord and went out into the rainy street.

Considering it was a Sunday Barry had been in remarkably good spirits, it was a pity it hadn't rubbed off on her. If she was not careful she would get like Markham, with nothing in her life but work. It was time to extend her social circle.

The streets were quiet, everyone else was with their families. What would Carlos have done on a Sunday afternoon? The Pink Elephant did not remain open. Listened to music on his expensive equipment maybe? But which of those they had interviewed was responsible for his death? It had to be one of them.

Following Ian's instructions they had surprised Sebastian Roberts by turning up at nine thirty on Sunday morning, time enough to have a private chat before he opened up. He was already showered and dressed when they rang the bell of the side door and he had invited them in without hesitation.

If he wondered why they were investigating his finances, he did not show it. 'It was my dream,' he had told them, 'and when this opportunity came up my parents lent me money to go with what I'd already saved. That way I could afford a larger down-payment and the bank fixed me up with the rest. If business continues the way it is there won't be any problems paying it back.'

'And the extension?'

'I went to Pollock's firm. His reputation's good around here. He quoted me a very reasonable price and told me not to worry, he'd be able to sort out any necessary planning permission. It was all arranged quickly and efficiently. Well, you've been downstairs, you can see what a good job they've done.'

'And in return?' Brenda wanted to know.

Roberts's frown was answer enough. 'What do you mean?'

'Presumably you owe him a favour now?'

'If I do, there's been no mention of it. I hope you're not implying there's anything illegal about this business, because I can assure you I wouldn't have touched it if there was. Look, I know you've got a job to do, but having one of my customers murdered and the police here all the time isn't going to help me. If I knew anything else about Chaz I'd've told you. He was just one of those people who kept to himself. If it'll put your minds at rest, you have my permission to go over any or all of my papers relating to my financial state. You can even speak to my bank manager if you want.'

'That won't be necessary,' Barry had told him. 'Sorry to have bothered you again.'

Brenda, as she glanced at the autumn clothes in a shop window, thought it might be that the Pink Elephant was being used as a meeting place for things Roberts knew nothing about. He had come across as basically honest and they already knew he was a hard worker, desperate to make a go of things.

At home, in the small, modern house she did not particularly like but which was all she could afford after she and Harry had divided the proceeds from the sale of their previous house, waiting for her to peruse them were brochures and pamphlets obtained from the public library containing all that Rickenham Green had to offer in the way of entertainment, further education, sporting activities and various clubs where like-minded people shared an interest. The hours made joining things difficult. She slung the brochures on the floor, took off her shoes and put her feet on the coffee table.

8

The first of the lab reports arrived on Monday morning. All negative. Charles Carlos's remains were free from illegal substances and any symptoms of illness. But, Ian thought, negatives were also useful as they ruled out certain possibilities; in this case revenge if he had passed on some disease or if he had double-crossed some drug dealer or threatened to expose him. So what now?

He picked up the typescript of the latest interview with Sebastian Roberts, read it quickly and threw it back on the desk in disgust. Pollock must have had a reason for going out of his way to help the man; if they asked him he would, of course, deny it or come up with something plausible.

'Where's the gen on Dawson?'

Barry looked up. 'He wasn't in. Didn't the late shift see him?'

'Apparently not. Where does he work?'

'I don't know.'

'Jesus Christ. What's the matter with everyone lately? He was brought in, questioned in an interview room in connection with a murder and a disappearance and we don't even know where he works? Who was responsible?'

Barry went downstairs to find out. 'Brown,' he said, 'late shift.'

'Right.' Ian made a note to speak to him. Rumours had reached him that Brown was slipping, that possibly he was hitting the bottle a bit too hard. Accepted, a drink was welcome after a stressful day or long hours on the go, but Ian, much as he loved a few pints himself, never let it interfere with the job. 'Get round to Dawson's address and bring him in. If he's not there, find him. And take someone with you.'

Carol was not sure how she had got through Sunday but one thing was certain: whatever the outcome, the truth had to be told however it might affect her future.

It was with a sense of relief that she set off for work on Monday morning, knowing she was about to do the right thing. It had not been easy to accept any of what she had been told but that was probably because she was so uncomplicated herself.

The car refused to start initially. She had stupidly parked it facing into the direction of the wind which had carried the rain with it. She got out and sprayed all the parts which were visible, waited a few minutes and tried the ignition again. Success.

Pools of water lay in the ruts in the track. There had not been enough rain for it to penetrate the ground. The fields had suffered in the same way, water had run off them instead of feeding the thirsty crops.

She parked in her usual spot and used the lift to reach her office. It was nine fifteen. One or two urgent matters were awaiting her attention. Conscientiously these were attended to first before she felt she deserved some coffee.

The internal telephone rang and made her start. Someone called Leon Dawson was asking to see her. The name meant nothing. She gave instructions for him to be shown up. 'Hello, I'm Carol Barnes. How can I help you?' She had not set eyes on him before but guessed, from his build, that he might be in construction work.

Leon had thought long and hard about Nigel's methods of operating. Selby was on the council, Selby got things done as far as planning decisions went, therefore, he concluded, Selby had a contact within the planning department and that contact would not be the office tea girl. Leon, however, did not have inside knowledge of how the system worked.

He stood with his hands resting on the edge of her desk,

116

leaning over towards her. Carol felt a moment's fear before thinking how nervous she had become. There were other people around and the man could not help how he looked.

'Have a seat, please. What is it you want?'

'You're in charge here?'

'Yes, but I don't make decisions, Mr Dawson, we have committees for that.'

'It's not a decision I want. I want to know where Bruce Selby is.'

She blanched but regained enough composure to answer in a steady voice, 'I honestly don't know.' At that moment it was true. Bruce had promised to clear things up by the time she got home; right now he might still be there or he could be in the car on his way to see his mother or the police. She felt her surroundings closing in. It was as if she no longer inhabited the real world but was watching herself from a distance. Who was this man and how much did he know? 'Are you from the police?'

'No. Let's just say I'm a friend of a friend.'

Through the window of the fifth-floor office she saw clouds roll away to reveal an ever widening patch of blue. A ray of light slanted on to the papers on her desk and over her hand, showing up the blue veins raised with tiredness. Dawson leant closer. Carol, who had taken a course in self-awareness, was no stranger to body language. She was terrified. 'I can't help you, I'm afraid. You'll have to excuse me, I'm due at a meeting in ten minutes.'

Dawson hesitated but he could not make a scene here. It didn't matter, he had got what he came for. Carol Barnes may not have known where Selby was at the precise moment he asked her but she would lead him to him, of that he was certain.

Elizabeth Selby was again resting when Brenda Gibbons returned. It was understandable, at her age the disappearance of her son would take its toll. She probably feared he was dead and coming to terms with a child dying before you was one of the

117

hardest things to endure. Norma Selby's manner was less vital than on previous visits, but the atmosphere in the house would affect them all.

'The children are staying with friends,' she said. 'I thought it best. Elizabeth's got enough to contend with without their noise.'

'How is Mrs Selby?'

'She could be better. Damn Bruce, why has he done this to us?' Norma sat down and wrapped her arms around herself as if she was cold. 'It might sound daft in this day and age but we really were a happy family until this happened. I don't think things will ever be the same again.'

'I need to ask a couple more questions. You mentioned Patti Evans, were there any other women?'

'None that he brought back here. Elizabeth always thought he might be discreetly visiting prostitutes, but I doubt it, it's not Bruce's style. He takes females out for dinner sometimes, family friends, or friends of friends, but my feeling is that he's not that interested. I've met men like it before, asexual, content as they are.'

'You don't think he might be interested in men?'

'What on earth are you suggesting?' Brenda turned around. Elizabeth Selby stood with one hand on the handle of the door. 'I heard the bell, I rather hoped it would be good news, I certainly didn't expect to hear that kind of remark in my house.'

'I'm afraid unpleasant questions have to be asked. Your son was last seen in a pub which is frequented by gays.'

'I read the papers, young lady, I was not unaware of that fact but he was talking to the proprietor no doubt. I happen to know Bruce was on the committee which passed the planning permission for the extension. I really can't imagine why you'd think my son had anything to do with *those* people. Have you seen them?'

'Yes. All the customers have been questioned. You seem to have strong views, Mrs Selby, considering our enlightened times.'

A noise, almost a snort, preceded her words. 'Enlightened does not mean better. I happen to be one of the old school, and proud of it. Things were a lot different when I was a girl. I was sorry when the law changed.'

Very strong views, Brenda thought, for a woman whom, if she was to be believed, it would not affect either way. 'We are in the process of speaking to everyone on the council again.'

'I should hope so. They are Bruce's contemporaries, he might well have confided in someone or told them where he was going. There'll be some woman behind it. Bruce is weak, easily led. I would offer you coffee, Constable, but I'm exhausted with all this. You'll have to excuse me.'

Constable. Mrs Selby had made her point.

'Sorry about that. You're not the only one, she's put us all through it. To be honest, that was really the reason I sent the children away, she was becoming quite nasty to them. Maurice and I realise she's no longer young and we make our excuses for her.'

'How old is she?'

'Sixty-seven.'

Not old at all by today's standards, Brenda thought, and she could have passed for a couple of years younger.

'I don't suppose you're allowed to tell me, but are you getting anywhere with finding him?'

'To be honest, no. But by this evening we may have jogged a few memories.'

'I do apologise for my mother-in-law's rudeness,' Norma said when she showed Brenda to the door.

'It's all right, I've been subjected to far worse than that.' She did not add that Harry had been one of the worst culprits.

Leon Dawson was still not to be found but officers had been despatched to speak to everyone who was at the council meeting that night and anyone else Selby would have had contact with during the course of his duties. No one had anything to add; they only reiterated that it was unlike Bruce to act unthinkingly.

119

'Who else would he deal with?' Markham asked the deputy leader.

'One or two full-timers at the Town Hall – we all do, of course.'

'Anyone in particular?'

'I can't say for sure. Bruce is not a great conversationalist. He'd probably know Carol Barnes, she's head of planning, because he was into that side of things. God knows why, I find it the least interesting part. Still, we can't all be the same.'

Markham's face had not shown a flicker of interest when he heard the name but here was yet another coincidence. It was Carol Barnes to whom he had spoken regarding the properties in Railway Terrace. His mouth tightened. He was getting as bad as the rest of them: it had not crossed his mind to ask her then if she knew Selby, but they had not at that time known that Selby and Pollock were connected and the incidents were still being treated separately. Carol Barnes next, then.

It was four o'clock and she had left work. 'At this time?' Markham wanted to know.

'She was in at eight,' one of her assistants told him. 'She often is, flexi-time, she saves up her hours to make a long weekend occasionally. She said she had something important to attend to today.'

'I'll need her home address.'

'I'm not sure that . . . ' The young man hesitated but recognised the fact that Markham was not going to leave without it.

'One of them has to have done it,' DCI Roper repeated. 'And now we've got this Barnes woman, no doubt she's involved somewhere along the line.' Carol Barnes had not been at home and there was no sign of a car, which was the only way to reach her property as buses didn't run that way. 'Don't tell me she's gone missing too. There seems to be a mass bloody exodus from this town. What we can't afford is to have a repeat of the Yorkshire Ripper business. How many times did they have him in before he was charged?' It was all there, he knew it was. The

120

whole set-up, the cast of characters, yet none of them seemed to be shielding anyone else.

Roberts's paperwork was, as he had claimed, beyond reproach. A quiet word with the bank manager, despite what he had been told, revealed that Roberts was gradually paying back a loan and, so far, that's where most of his profit went. There were no enormous amounts of money involved. The bank manager, whom Ian knew well enough to elicit such information from on an informal basis, also told him that he had met Mr and Mrs Roberts when they came in to sign some papers and that they had lent their son money with an interest-free arrangement.

Leon Dawson had a background of violence but would he be so stupid as to admit he couldn't stand Carlos if he had killed him? Not stupid, Ian realised, but perhaps clever, to divert attention away from himself.

And, to cap it all, a young couple had turned up to say they had been away for the weekend and had only just read the *Herald* and that they had been down by the stream at the time the woman with her two children had heard their argument. They had seen her holding a little boy's hand as he paddled in the water, shallow after the weeks of sunshine.

'Get me Pollock.'

'Please,' Barry muttered as he looked up the number prior to dialling it.

Ian almost snatched the phone from him when he was put through by Pollock's secretary. 'You're lucky to catch me in the office,' he said. 'I was just about to go home.'

'Does the name Leon Dawson mean anything to you?'

'Of course it does, he works for me. And he uses the Elephant. What's this all about, Chief Inspector?'

'I'd rather not discuss it over the telephone. Can you call in at the station on your way home?'

'We've got visitors ... no, all right, it'll be easier that way.' Pollock realised they would only come out to the house if he refused and Anne-Marie was worried enough already. 'I'll ring my wife and come straight over.'

121

'He works for him,' Ian said with grim satisfaction. He added the name to his diagram and filled in two more arrows linking Dawson to both Pollock and the Pink Elephant. 'Pretty, isn't it? If only we knew what it meant.'

Pollock was wearing mud-smeared boots and a lightweight jacket. Although the sun had continued to shine throughout the day, building sites would still be puddled and messy. Ian had been waiting for him downstairs and showed him into his office. An interview room would not intimidate this man.

'You obviously suspect Dawson of something – may I ask what it is? Or is it a case of him helping you with your inquiries, as I believe you lot like to phrase it?'

'The latter. How long has Dawson worked for you?'

'About seven or eight years. It's all legal, stamps, tax, the lot, and he's got his ticket. And before you ask, I know about his past, but it was a long time ago, water under the bridge. I warned him when I took him on, any trouble and he's out before he can protest.'

'Hard worker?'

'He is. He's one of those adaptable types, can turn his hand to anything and he doesn't whinge. He's on my payroll and he's happy with that, does anything I ask him.'

'Anything?'

'What's that supposed to mean?'

'Nothing, just a thought. Where is he now?'

'At home. In the pub. How should I know?'

'Where was he today?'

Pollock thought about it. 'He drove some supplies out to one of my sites first thing. Then he had an hour or so off before coming back to make a few more deliveries.'

'What vehicle does he use?'

'One of mine, can't miss them.' Pollock grinned. The logo of his companies was intended not to be missed.

'Does he have use of it in his own time?'

'No. None of them do. I pay well and treat the men fairly but there are limits.'

'Is it possible he could've taken one without your knowledge?'

'Anything's possible, but it's highly unlikely. They're all parked up every night, locked inside the fencing of whichever site is applicable.'

And they had already ascertained that Dawson did not possess transport of his own. But why were they assuming transport was needed? Supposing Carlos had been down by the river with his killer by choice, taking a walk, talking, or perhaps for sex with someone who could not afford to let it be known which way his inclinations lay, a married man, say. It would not be the first time. Carlos, knowing the strong position he was in, might have threatened blackmail and been murdered for his efforts. Ian sighed. In which case the field was suddenly wide open again.

'Something troubling you?'

'Many things trouble me, Mr Pollock, but this case does especially. Carol Barnes.' He started again.

'Yes, I know Carol. Not my type, but an efficient, no-nonsense sort of woman.'

'How do you know her?'

'I make it my business to know anyone who's in the right place and to keep on the right side of them.'

'She has influence?'

'Not influence, no. Another thing, in case it crossed your mind, I know Dawson's gay. And that doesn't bother me either. You'd be amazed how many of them are strapping great lads. He's not overtly so, he wouldn't last in the trade if he was, and if the others know, they leave him alone.'

'Do you socialise with either Dawson or Barnes?'

'No. I'm not that foolish. I see Leon in the pub sometimes, exchange a few words, not that he's ever got much to say. Is that it?'

'Bruce Selby knows Miss Barnes too.'

'Of course he does. I really can't see what you're getting at.'

Neither could Ian but he was desperate. By throwing in all the names he had hoped to get a reaction of some sort. Pollock stood up to leave. 'How did you get started, Mr Pollock? I mean what was it that enabled you to become so wealthy today?'

'Now look here, I find that suggestion offensive. I did it the hard way. All right, my methods weren't always by the book, I'll admit that, and I took chances, made out I already had money, that's the only way to get anyone to lend you any, and it paid off. Perhaps things weren't always quite as they should be but I can assure you nothing I did would have put me in jail. Nor does anything I do now. I think I've answered enough of your questions and my wife will be expecting me home before our guests arrive. Goodnight, Roper.'

That's telling me, he thought as he remained, motionless, behind his desk. It was Roper now, and Pollock had made it quite clear he had friends and money and a wife waiting for him whereas he, Roper, would probably be stuck here until late.

He might have sat there for ages had not Barry Swan come bursting in. His face was white and his features seemed to have shrunk. 'I've got to go, Ian. It's Lucy. She tripped down the stairs.'

'Is she badly hurt?'

'I don't know. It's not that, it's the baby. I'll ring later.'

'The baby?' Ian stared into the empty corridor outside his open door. Of course, that's why he had been so jubilant over the weekend. For ten minutes his thoughts were with the Swans. They must have only just known about the child and now they might lose it. How would he have felt if it had been Moira? More concerned for her, he knew that with certainty. There might always be another baby, there would never be another Moira.

Elizabeth Selby was tired of waiting for news of Bruce. It was enervating just sitting around waiting for the telephone to ring or another visit from the police. She told Norma she was going out and would be gone some time. She did not add that she was going to the Elms Golf and Country Club hoping to make up a foursome and that she might even treat herself to dinner there if she could find an entertaining enough companion. Norma would no doubt think her callous but Norma respected her privacy and would not ask where she was going.

One or two would drift in after work. It was still light enough to play up until eight. Her golfing clothes were kept in a locker and her clubs were in the boot of the car so there was no need for any preparations. She also kept toilet things there in case she wanted a shower afterwards. Her dress, lilac and grey print with a silver belt, was suitable for the members' dining-room. After applying fresh lipstick she left the house.

As she drove she wondered again where Bruce was holed up. That was how she thought of it. He was not dead, she was certain. Bruce would never take his own life and he was so dull he was not capable of arousing anyone enough to take it for him. During his boyhood, if he had done something wrong and was afraid of the punishment she might mete out to him, he would hide in the wardrobe or the garden shed or huddle amongst the rhododendron bushes at the end of the garden but where he was taking refuge now she could not imagine. He'd come home, like a bad penny, when whoever was sheltering him got bored with him.

Leon Dawson went back to take a lorry load of breeze blocks to one of Pollock's sites. Unloading took longer than he had anticipated but he was back outside the Town Hall precinct by three forty-five. This time he was driving a dark blue Bedford van in which were carefully stacked panes of glass to be delivered to a client who was having a conservatory built. The job wasn't urgent, as long as it was done that day, because the carpenters had not yet finished erecting the framework. If he didn't arrive until seven it would make no difference.

Carol Barnes hurried across the paved area interspersed with trees and headed for the underground car-park. Her head was up but she did not look happy. Leon turned the ignition key, still keeping an eye out for traffic wardens or policemen because he was illegally parked. Allowing a car to overtake him he pulled out once Carol had indicated left and joined the main road. Several miles later he had to drop back. Little traffic used the

B-road out to Frampton but he only saw her eyes in the rear view mirror at the appropriate times. She was not aware she was being followed. When she turned into a gate and came to a stop he continued on past until he found a space to turn around then headed back to Rickenham Green and delivered the glass. The problem was, how did he get himself back out here later after he had returned the van? If buses ran, and that was doubtful, he had not noticed any stops, he might be remembered by the driver, not that he intended doing anything illegal, but he did not want any complications. His only intention in life was to keep on the right side of Nigel Pollock, to do him a favour. Pollock was the only person in his life who had taken him at face value and did not make judgements other than on his abilities as an employee. For the first time ever Leon Dawson had gained some self-respect. He had already returned the Bedford when Pollock received the call from DCI Roper.

At the bus station he checked all the timetables; nothing went out that way, not even near enough for him to get off and walk. 'To hell with it,' he said. Why was he being so cagey, he wasn't doing anything wrong?

He walked to the taxi rank and gave the driver directions. 'I don't know the exact address, but I know how to get there.'

'It'll cost you six quid.'

'And if I get you to wait and bring me back?'

'I'll do it for a tenner.'

Leon got into the back seat. If he sat in the front the driver might start making conversation and he wanted to think about what he would actually do if the Barnes woman did tell him where Selby was. It had been an inspired guess that Selby would know the head of the planning department, but her reaction had given more away than she intended. Perhaps there was even something going on between the two of them.

'This'll do,' Leon said as they approached a gateway where the taxi would not obstruct other traffic. 'I shan't be long.' All he meant to do was to give her a fright. He knew where she lived, and it was an isolated spot, she was sure to tell him what he wanted to know.

As he approached the cottage he heard raised voices. He stopped and listened. Bingo. Selby was there with her. Unable to see a bell or knocker, he crashed his fist against the front door. There was silence. He knocked again before he heard high heels on the floor.

'Oh.' Carol raised her hands as if to ward off a blow.

'We meet again, Ms Barnes. Can I speak to Selby?'

'He's not here.'

'Really? You make a habit of arguing with yourself, do you, impersonating his voice?'

'No, look, I don't know what . . .' Leon pushed past her and there in the kitchen, quivering like a whipped child, was Bruce.

'I told you you should've done what I said,' Carol told him. 'This has gone too far. I will not have this sort of thing happening to me. I don't know what you want,' she turned to address Leon, 'but if you don't leave my property right now I shall call the police.' She hoped she sounded braver and more authoritative than she felt.

'I don't think you will, otherwise they'll find old Brucie, won't they? Mr Pollock was asking after you.'

'Was he?' Bruce's voice was low. 'What did he want?'

'He was wondering where you'd got to, that's all. I thought I'd let him know.'

'You don't frighten me, you know.' Leon let that one pass. 'Just get out of here, you're trespassing.'

'You're coming with me.'

'No.' Leon advanced towards him. 'Get away from me.' Bruce stood up, knocking the chair over as he did so. 'Stay away, do you hear? I saw you, I know what happened.' His voice was now several octaves higher.

Carol watched with disgust. Surely Bruce could act with a bit more dignity. Dawson was certainly intimidating but if he had meant them any harm he would have acted by now. Besides, it didn't look as if he was armed. Once more it was time for her to

127

take control. 'You're wrong, you know. If you leave now I won't call the police, but Mr Selby and I will go into Rickenham immediately and make his whereabouts known. As you were supposed to have done this morning,' she added for Bruce's benefit. Had he done so they would not have been subjected to this violent interruption.

'I'll tell them,' Bruce said. 'I'll tell them everything.'

Leon's eyes narrowed. What on earth was the man whimpering about? He had simply wanted to find him for Nigel's sake. And then he understood. He swore. There was no doubt how the police would react. They'd take Selby's side. Selby was a professional man and came from a wealthy family. Selby did not have a record. But he would not try to stop him, he dare not take the chance. If he hit him, which he badly wanted to do, placing a well-aimed fist in that pudgy stomach and thereby winding him, it would make matters worse. Pollock knew about his previous offence and had warned him in no uncertain terms that a repeat was not something to be contemplated. To ignore the warning would be to lose everything he had gained.

'Make sure you do,' he growled, 'or I'll tell them for you.'

'You took your time.' The taxi driver was annoyed. He should have left the deal a little more fluid. He had thought his passenger merely wanted to deliver something, not stay for dinner. Still, he did not look like the sort to argue with, especially out here with no witnesses.

When Leon returned to his flat he did not have a chance to enter it. Before he was aware what was happening his head was being forced down as he was bundled into the back of an unmarked car and he was on his way to Rickenham Green headquarters.

'Well, Bruce?'

Bruce had sagged into a kitchen chair. 'I didn't do it, Carol. I swear it.'

'I'm not sure I believe you any longer.' She took the chair

128

opposite. It had been a lie, the whole thing had been a deliberate attempt to deceive her. It saddened her. For several months she had thought Bruce was the one person she would be willing to spend her life with; a man who shared the same interests and who enjoyed the quiet life. He had come to her with some ridiculous excuse about Pollock putting the pressure on, an excuse she had chosen to believe because Pollock was a powerful man, although she had not seen how because, alone, Bruce was not in any position to do him favours.

'I've been so stupid,' she admitted, watching the face of the man she had come to love crumple. 'I believed all that nonsense about your family, too.' He had told her that he wasn't ready to introduce her to them for fear of his mother putting her off. 'I'm very fond of her,' he had said, 'but she does tend to act the lady of the manor and she lives in the past. I was afraid she might look down on you for going out and earning your own living.'

It had sounded feeble at the time; how much feebler it seemed now. Bruce had used her as a means of avoiding answering any questions the police wished to ask him. He had treated her home as no more than a hide-out and thus sullied it. What puzzled her now was why he was hiding. If, as he claimed, he had seen Dawson attack the man who was killed, why hadn't he gone straight to the police and told them? Why go into hiding when he would be found at some point? She could have unwittingly given him away at any time. Something did not ring true. Carol knew Bruce was lying about his family and about the real reason he was using her.

'That's blown that theory out of the window.' Ian leant against one of the desks in the control room. The floor was littered with box files which contained statements and any other information pertaining to the case. All the suspects seemed to know one another but the computer could not come up with a connection. Ian had a gut feeling that facts were being withheld but no one was actually lying.

*

It was dusk, almost dark, when PC Stone had radioed in from his patrol car. He and Jackson were covering the town centre that evening, Stone driving, Jackson philosophising from the passenger seat when he had suddenly stopped talking and looked back in the wing mirror. 'Pull in,' he said calmly. They got out of the car and walked thirty or forty yards back up the street. It had been the flame of a lighter which had caught his eye, too low down for someone to be lighting a cigarette.

Two boys in their early teens had their backs to the entrance to the yard so did not see Stone and Jackson watching them, waiting to make sure they were not mistaken as to what they were doing. Rubbish was stacked against the wall of a shoe shop, no doubt containing a high percentage of inflammable material if they chucked out the boxes customers did not want. A blaze took hold. The boys turned, about to run, when they realised their exit was blocked. They dashed for the wall but it was too high for them to climb. PC Stone, younger and fitter, remained in the entrance to the yard whilst Jackson quickly kicked the rubbish away until it was in a position where it could do no more harm. There was a small fire extinguisher in the patrol car but fetching it might mean one of the youths escaped. 'It's safe enough,' he said. 'Come on, boys, a nice little ride then we'll let your parents know where you are.'

'So why did it stop?' Ian asked when he had been informed.

'Seems the older one was on holiday with his parents and the other one wasn't brave enough to start fires on his own. They got back a couple of days ago. There was one we missed.' DC Gibbons waved the report of the earlier fire under his nose. 'Not much of a future for them, is there?'

The boys were aged thirteen and fourteen and they had been in trouble before, although not for similar offences. 'I know what I'd do with them,' Ian said.

In mitigation they claimed they had not known anyone lived over the TV and video repair shop and, having seen it for himself, Markham could see why. The business may have been run down but the upstairs was a disgrace with its peeling paintwork and filthy, ragged nets, and there had been no lights on as the owners were out. The shop in Railway Terrace had been a matter of chance. They had been hanging around down by the railway when they'd seen the Matthews leave, locking up behind them. Had they been at home they would not have dared go in through the back gate. They had hoped there would be something worth stealing but when they found only junk and no way to break into the premises because the store-room window was protected with metal bars, they had started a fire instead. But they refused to admit they were responsible for damaging Mrs Mostyn's property. As all the other incidents had occurred in the absence of people it was likely they were telling the truth.

'What if we're wrong about everything? What if none of the things we've investigated has any relevance?' It was unlike the Chief to be so pessimistic. At least they had plenty to work on now.

Ian rubbed his chin. The bristles were tough and starting to show through. He would like to be at home, with Moira pouring him a drink. And then the telephone rang.

'Leon Dawson's been brought in,' the desk sergeant informed him. 'He's in interview room 5.'

As soon as he replaced it, it rang again. 'It's me, Barry. I won't be back tonight. They're keeping Lucy in. She's still bleeding, but they haven't given up hope of saving the baby. I'll come in first thing though.' He hadn't given Barry a thought. What a thing to happen, before the word had got around and anyone had had a chance to congratulate the couple. Perhaps it was as well if all that was to follow was commiserations. It was hard going, Barry out of action, Alan Campbell away on his blasted course, Winston Emmanuel no longer with them. Correction, he told himself, DC Gibbons is just as, if not more, efficient. Should he allow her to interview Dawson? She might get a better reaction than another male.

Unbelievably, before he came to a decision, the phone went for the third time. 'Sorry to bother you again, sir, but Bruce Selby and Carol Barnes have just arrived.'

9

Lucy Swan lay in her high hospital bed trying not to cry. There was no pain, the doctor had seen to that, but until now she had not known just how much she wanted the baby. She hadn't lost it yet but she was preparing herself for the worst. The bottom end of the bed was raised on blocks and she had been injected with heaven knew what. And there was Barry to worry about. He looked awful and near to tears himself. In fact, she decided, she would be better off if he went home.

'I'm very tired,' she said tactfully. 'It might be best if I sleep.'

Barry squeezed her hand. Five years ago if anyone had told him he would feel this way about a woman and the child she was carrying he would have laughed. He did not want to leave but Lucy's face was grey. 'You'll be all right.' He kissed her forehead, not knowing what else to say. 'I'll ring first thing in the morning.'

She smiled but did not tell him that it might be the hospital who rang him first.

Out in the vast car-park he could not remember where he had put the car. Immediately the call had come through to the station his one thought had been to get there. Now it was much emptier, visiting time was over although on many wards there were no longer any restrictions. He could not face the flat and decided to go back to work.

Half-way into town he turned around. He had to go home, suppose Lucy wanted him or something worse happened. It was, he thought later, the longest night of his life. It was dawn before he closed his eyes and fell asleep in the chair.

*

'All we need is for Pollock to waltz in,' Ian commented in amazement. 'I suggest we give them a little time before we speak to them.' It was an old trick. It made people more eager to talk if they were kept waiting because, whatever they had to say, they wanted to get it over with quickly. The other side, though, was that the police wanted to hear what they had to say. 'Coffee all round, I think.' The bad mood was dissipating. He left the control room long enough to let Moira know he would not be home yet for a while. 'You go to bed. No need to wait up. It'll be the small hours the way things are going here.'

'Good news?'

'We don't know yet.'

'I will go up if you're not here by eleven. I've got work tomorrow and Mark and Lara are coming.'

He had forgotten. That was all he needed if he was going to be up half the night. Still, if they got what they wanted he would take the morning off.

'OK, Brenda, you take Dawson, I'll speak to Selby. Make it formal, have a PC in with you. Male.' He saw a flash of something in her eyes. 'No offence meant.' She had learnt how to handle herself at training college. 'Just so's *he* knows. You'll be the one asking the questions.'

'Yes, sir.' She left the room with a very straight back.

Carol Barnes had been put in a separate room and given a cup of coffee and a magazine to read, both of which she ignored. She blamed herself and began to wonder if she had left herself open to some criminal charge. For now all she could do was wait.

'Mr Selby. We meet at last.'

Bruce looked up. He was a mess and could easily pass for older than his given age. There was a faint odour of stale sweat and he was sweating at the moment, his face shone under the harsh, overhead light.

Ian decided to go in gently. There was, after all, the slightest chance Selby had been unaware they were looking for him.

134

'I did know,' he admitted. 'What will happen to me?'

'That remains to be seen. First and foremost, why did you disappear and put your family through so much anguish?'

'I had to. I was frightened.'

'Of whom, or what?'

'Everyone.'

'I think you'll have to make yourself clearer than that.'

'It was what I saw.' Bruce pulled himself upright from his slumped position. The look on his face told Ian he had come to some sort of decision but whether it was to tell the whole story or to lie remained to be seen. 'That night, that night in the Elephant, I was there. Chaz was there too. I didn't like him, I took a dislike to him the first time he spoke to me and I've avoided him ever since. But I didn't kill him. And then, well, you see, you might think I had reason to.'

'Why might I think that, Mr Selby?'

'Because of the photograph. Someone took a picture, Chaz did it on purpose, I'm quite certain of that.'

'Did what?'

'There was a party of some sort going on. I was standing at the bar talking to Mr Pollock when Chaz suddenly came up to me and put his arm around me. When I looked up the flashbulb went off. I think he may have wanted to use it to blackmail me.'

'So you killed him.'

'No.' Selby's voice rose in panic. 'Can't you see, that's exactly what I thought you'd think.'

'So you ran away and hid, waiting for the culprit to be caught. Hardly the actions of a good citizen, especially someone in your position.'

'I know.' He bowed his head. 'I do know that. But Carol, well, she said I could stay there and I didn't know what my family would think if they believed I was in any way involved.'

'You do realise how much of our time and money you've wasted, time that could be spent on people who really need it.'

'I'm sorry. Look, I can make a donation . . .'

'We don't accept bribes, Mr Selby. Maybe it works that way in the planning world, maybe bribes and blackmail are the norm, but not here.' Ian watched to see what reaction this would produce. Harsh words, but possibly true ones. Bruce Selby stared at him. The pale grey pupils in their yellowish whites showed nothing but incomprehension.

'Bribes? Who's been taking bribes?'

Ian sat back and rested his forearms on the desk, hands clasped. 'I thought you'd tell *me* that.'

'I don't understand. I thought this was to do with Chaz's murder.'

'It might all be one and the same thing. How much does Pollock pay you, or what do you have to do so he won't spill the beans?'

'Pollock? What's he got to do with anything?' There was no doubt the confusion was genuine.

'Railway Terrace? The Pink Elephant?' Ian paused. 'Patti Evans?'

Selby groaned. 'Not Patti, please don't bring her into it.'

'It's a bit late for that. We've spoken to her. Had you come forward as requested it would not have been necessary.'

'Her husband, does he know?'

Ian decided to let him suffer. 'That is not what we're here to discuss. Now tell me about the bribes.'

'There aren't any. All those things, they were all above board.'

'Oh, really?'

'You don't understand how it works.'

'Strange, I thought I had a fairly good knowledge of local government. However, if you'd care to enlighten me . . . You see, I find it odd that the brewery were refused planning permission for an extension yet Mr Roberts, who happens to know both yourself and Pollock, succeeded.'

'Chief Inspector, it was simply that they weren't that bothered. The business was going downhill and no publican wanted to take it on. Let me explain.'

'Please do.'

'If anyone wants to build or make alterations or add an exten-

136

sion they first have to apply to the planning department. If it's a small job, like Sebastian's extension, an officers' committee from the planning department can say yes or no. The brewery was refused permission after much consideration because of a great deal of lobbying by the public. The place was an eyesore and local residents had enough problems with it as it was. The brewery, as I said, had, by that time, decided to cut their losses and did not bother to appeal. The council committee, as opposed to the planning department committee, can overrule any decisions made by the planning officers, and they don't have to give any reasons why. Am I making this clear?' Selby was not being sarcastic, his tone implied he was worried his interrogator would not understand the nuances of planning. Ian nodded. 'There are ways around it, but really, they're mostly a waste of time. If a potential applicant knows an influential councillor they can lobby him or her, but they would need to be extremely influential to get the rest of the committee to go along with whatever's required. I have never known it happen in my time.'

'So where does Carol Barnes come into it?'

'She doesn't, not in the way you're suggesting. We met, naturally, through our respective jobs, and we formed a relationship. There's no way she could be involved in anything like that because decisions made by her team can be overruled.'

'And Pollock?' He had to ask although he felt everything was slipping away from him, that they had been on the wrong track all along.

'Pollock enjoys knowing the right people. He likes other people to think he can pull strings. He has no need to. His business affairs are straight, well, I expect you've looked into that, and the work his firm does is excellent. He uses me, and possibly Miss Barnes, as his ears. He hopes we'll tell him what the opposition is up to before it reaches the press.' Selby managed a weak smile. 'In my experience the press seem to know what's going on before the committee has reached a decision. I'm quite sure Pollock stores up information against a rainy day.'

'You mean if his company should ever go under he could then

137

pull those strings, remind people of favours owed or perhaps threaten to expose their seamier sides?'

'Yes, but I'm only guessing.'

Ian noticed how relaxed Selby had become, and he had allowed it to happen by getting him on to his favourite subject. If all that he said was true, then surely the fear of Chaz using that photograph was exaggerated. A man like Selby could laugh it off or produce Carol Barnes as proof that he was not homosexual. Yet Brenda Gibbons had said that Norma Selby believed him to be asexual whereas Brenda herself was of the opinion that he either preferred the company of men or was bisexual. What must Carol Barnes think? If these differences of opinion were to be taken seriously Selby must have one hell of an identity crisis on his hands.

'Back to Charles Carlos. Why would he want to blackmail you? What could you possibly do for him?'

'Money, I suppose.'

'Mr Selby, forgive me for not accepting what you say, but I find it hard to believe that anyone, especially yourself, would go into hiding, create all that misery for your family, and still refuse to come forward when you know perfectly well we wanted to speak to you. It was your mother who reported you missing otherwise we might not have even been aware you knew the victim. Can't you see what a hole you've dug for yourself? Not forgetting what this might do to Patti Evans's marriage. Now, forgetting Pollock and the planning department, why did you do it?'

'I was scared. Terrified. Of what Chaz might do, yes, but it was more than that. Once I realised he'd been murdered I knew you'd think it was me if that picture came to light. I wanted to stay out of the way until you caught whoever did it.'

Ian inhaled deeply and lit a cigarette. 'Do you smoke, Mr Selby?' He had him. My God, the man had fallen straight into the trap.

'No.'

'All right. I wonder if you can explain how it is that you

138

disappeared on that Thursday, disappeared because, you say, Carlos had been murdered and we, through the photograph, might connect you to his death, even think you killed him,' Selby was leaning forward now, 'when his body was not found until the following Tuesday?'

There was a deathly silence. Selby leant on the table and put his head between his hands.

'Well?'

'It wasn't what you think.'

'Then you'd better tell me just how it was.' Ian glanced at the clock on the wall. He was taking great care not to interview him longer than was allowed. Soon the man would be entitled to food and drink if he required it, but from what had been recorded on the tape so far PACE regulations would allow for them to hold him.

'Mr Dawson, I'm going to organise some coffee. I need it even if you don't.' Brenda was tired and Dawson's aftershave was unpleasant.

Dawson had refused all offers of refreshment so far but this time, his mouth dry, he gave in. 'Yeah, I'll have a coffee.'

She left the interview room for only a couple of minutes. 'To make sure there are no errors, we'll go over it once more.' She meant, and he knew it, to see if she could catch him out. He had told the truth and he would continue to do so. His one mistake had been in not coming forward and admitting his part but, with his record, who would believe him? This detective was attractive and she was smart, but if they'd sent a female hoping she could disarm him, they were mistaken. Women did not interest him.

'So you saw Mr Carlos ask a man to take the photo of him and Mr Selby together, a photo that could be interpreted in a certain way if Mr Carlos so desired. You, being a loyal employee of Mr Pollock and knowing Mr Pollock was often in the company of Mr Selby, decided to get it off him.'

'Yes.'

139

'So you followed him out to the toilet, or that's where you thought he went, only to discover he had left by the back door. You asked for the picture and he refused to give it to you.'

'He was a slimebag. No one liked him. I hardly knew Selby, but he seemed all right. Quiet, but decent enough.'

'And? Mr Dawson?' Brenda saw there was more to come. 'You admit you hit Carlos.'

'Yes. Fairly hard. There was blood on his face and he fell to the ground. I could've killed him. I wanted to.' He stopped. Telling the rest of it might put suspicion on Nigel and that was the last thing he wanted to do. However, if they were digging that deep it was best to tell the truth. 'But it wasn't just that.'

Brenda felt some of the tension ease out of her muscles. Now they were getting down to it.

'What Chaz wanted was to be recognised by Nigel, he wanted to be on his payroll, like me. He kept boasting what he could do for him, how he knew ways to make things easier. But Nigel didn't want anything to do with him.'

'So you hit him to warn him off?'

'Partly, but also because of what he'd already done. I overheard what he said to Mr Pollock. Mr Pollock was so disgusted I thought he was going to hit him himself.'

'Why was that?'

'Because Chaz was aware that he was interested in purchasing all the houses in Railway Terrace, initially for the supermarket deal where he would have sold them the land then done the construction work himself. He'd have made a fortune. Well, that fell through. Mr Pollock still wanted the houses. He was going to pull them down and build luxury flats with integral garages; he could get around the parking restrictions that way, you see. He realised it was an up and coming area. Then when Chaz admitted what he had done he put things on hold. He warned him off, said if he heard any more about it, he would go to the police.'

'Heard any more about what?'

'About terrorising old ladies.'

140

'Mrs Mostyn?'

'I don't know the name. Some woman in Railway Terrace, so Chaz said.'

'And why didn't Pollock, if he's the paragon you make him out to be, tell us?'

'Because Chaz is . . . was a liar. We weren't sure if he was just saying it to impress or whether these things had actually happened. Mr Pollock also thought he might be taking the credit for someone else's vandalism. I don't mean credit,' he added hastily.

'It's all right.' She understood what he did mean and she also realised Mrs Mostyn's problems had stopped recently. If it had been down to Charles Carlos, that was another crime solved. 'Mr Pollock felt strongly about what he was up to, strongly enough to kill him?'

Leon's mouth dropped open. 'Nigel? You've got to be joking.'

'Or to get someone to do it for him?'

'No.' The word was emphatic. 'He just wouldn't. I, um . . .'

'Yes?'

Leon studied his fingernails; they were stained, his hands calloused. He had to work on the basis that Bruce Selby meant what he said, that he would tell the police what he had seen. Up to the time when he saw him at the Barnes woman's place, he had believed him to be a decent type and assumed his disappearance was unconnected with Chaz's death. He had radically changed his mind. He did not want to drop anyone in it, but Selby's evidence would provide his own alibi. 'I was seen. When I hit Chaz. Bruce Selby saw me do it. He'll be able to tell you that although I hit him, Chaz got up and walked away.'

'Did you threaten Mr Selby, is that why he disappeared?'

'No. I didn't know he'd seen me.'

Brenda allowed herself a few seconds to digest this piece of information. 'Mr Dawson, if you didn't see Mr Selby on that Thursday, how do you know *he* saw *you*?'

'He told me, earlier today.'

'Today?' What was going on out there? Whilst they, the police, had been chasing their tails, everyone else seemed completely aware of where the others were and what they were doing.

'I began to think he might know something about it. Mr Pollock was asking where he was. I thought I was being helpful. I saw Miss Barnes in her office and, well . . .' he shrugged, 'I put two and two together.' It was best not to say he had followed her. 'Mr Selby was at her place. He told me then.'

'Why didn't you come forward immediately then? You knew we wanted to speak to him.'

'I didn't have a chance. I got the taxi to drop me home and before I could have a wash I was pounced on and dragged into a car. I'd been at work all day, I didn't want to come here like this.' He indicated his clothing.

Brenda thought they would never know if that was what he had really intended but the rest of his story had the ring of truth. It would be interesting to compare it with Selby's version. Leon Dawson was allowed to leave but told to remain at his present address.

The pubs were closed by the time the suspects had been released but Markham said he knew where he could find a bottle. Brenda Gibbons said she would stick with coffee. The next shift had already come on and were up to date with developments but Ian and Brenda could not leave an interview half-way through and hand it over to someone else.

Markham rinsed several used plastic drinks cups in the sink and poured a drink for those who wanted one. The late shift looked on with envy.

'Their stories coincide in that Dawson whacked Carlos but Selby claims that Carlos didn't get up, that he saw Dawson kill him so he ran, to avoid getting mixed up in it, knowing Carlos had a photograph that could be interpreted as incriminating. He also claims he was sure Dawson saw him and was likely to come after him and mete out the same treatment. He is, as everyone says, weak, but so weak he couldn't even face coming here if what he thought he saw was true?'

'And the other thing, sir,' Brenda said, interrupting his flow of thought, 'is that no one knew about his relationship with Carol Barnes, not his family, no one. Why keep it a secret? Neither of them are married, or even vaguely attached elsewhere. I've told her we'll need to speak to her again tomorrow.'

'Where's Selby gone?'

'A car took him to his mother's.' This was from Markham.

'Good. That'll save her another sleepless night.' Ian knew about the joys of parenthood.

Markham, who had not been present during either interview, voiced his own opinion. 'If Selby's not lying, if Dawson did kill him somewhere round the back of the Elephant, how did he get the body down to the river? He hasn't got transport, we've checked, unless he borrowed, or stole, a car, and that would mean it was premeditated. I can't see it. If you want to knock someone off, you don't do it on the doorstep of a pub, especially one you both use.'

'I agree,' Ian said. 'Let's accept Dawson hit Carlos and Selby saw him. For reasons of his own; the photograph, jealousy, whatever, Selby decides to finish the job off. He *did* have transport that night, his car, with which he drove himself to Carol Barnes's place.'

'Well, we'll know soon enough. I'm going home.' Brenda dropped her coffee container into the bin and brushed back her hair. She looked tired, but not as weary as the Chief.

'Come on, Brenda's right.' Ian picked up his jacket and hooked it over his shoulder. Before Selby was released he had been asked to hand over his car keys and the key to the padlock on Carol's shed. Forensics had already collected the car. If the victim had been inside it, unless Selby had done a thorough cleaning job, they would find evidence to confirm it. Carol Barnes, he thought, had put her faith in the wrong man whether or not he was innocent. Someone other than himself would

143

decide her fate for concealing Selby's whereabouts and, for once, he was glad it was not up to him.

As quiet as he was, Ian still disturbed Moira which surprised him. 'It wasn't you,' she said. 'I keep thinking about how we're going to get through two weeks of Lara.'

'Right now young Lara's presence seems like a picnic.'

Moira did not ask if they had arrested anyone, there was no need. Ian's large, warm body was a comfort. She moved against him and closed her eyes. He lay still, knowing with absolute certainty they had got it all wrong.

It seemed obvious now – apart from Selby no one had refused to co-operate, no one really had anything to hide. If Carlos had simply left the Pink Elephant after Dawson had floored him and found a stranger to sympathise they might never know who murdered him. But Ian's money was on Selby.

'Toast?' Moira asked the next morning.

'Yes, just one piece. Back in a minute.'

She heard him make a brief telephone call. 'I feel awful about that, I should've rung last night. Barry,' he said, seeing she had no idea what he was talking about. 'Lucy's pregnant, she had a bad fall and was taken to hospital yesterday. I meant to ring him last night.' He paused. 'I should say was pregnant.'

'Oh, no, Ian. How is she?' Moira sat down, shocked – her guess had been correct.

'Sedated. He was just on his way to see her. I've told him I don't want to see him at the station today. What do I do, Moira?'

'Do?'

'I don't want to upset either of them, I mean, flowers wouldn't be appropriate, would they? From everyone.'

'No, they wouldn't.' She laid a hand on his arm. 'I think it's best to do nothing. Let them come to terms with it together.'

'But won't that seem as if we don't care?'

'Not if they hadn't told anyone yet. Wait until you speak to Barry face to face.'

'You're right.' He kissed her and went out into the early September sunlight forgetting to eat his toast.

Moira had a slight headache caused through lack of sleep. For Ian's sake she had pretended to drop off again. It was daft to worry about the consequences of the presence of a young woman under their roof but if there was an atmosphere, on top of what Ian had to contend with, she did not feel she could cope. And now this news. And a day's work ahead of her before Mark and Lara arrived. One minute at a time, she told herself as she slid Ian's cold toast into the pedal bin and hid the dishes in the washing-up bowl under the sink because there was not time to see to them and she did not want the kitchen looking a mess if Mark arrived before she got home.

'Where's Barry?' DC Gibbons asked several of her fellow officers as she made her way to the general office. No one seemed to know.

'He's taking some time off,' Ian told the assembled group. 'I can't say more than that.' Better to say something immediately than have everyone speculating. 'When he returns he may tell you the reason himself, but I'd prefer it if you didn't push him.'

Heads turned and eyebrows were raised. Swan could be an arrogant bastard but he didn't shirk. It had to be serious if it was in the middle of a major inquiry.

Despatched to various duties, most of them forgot about the absence of Barry Swan and not long into the day Ian received a message from John Cotton, head of Scene-of-Crime. 'Nothing conclusive yet,' he said, 'but already it looks as if Carlos was, at some point, a passenger in Selby's car. We've got a couple of hairs, fingerprints, and a cigarette end, Carlos's brand. Don't get too excited, none of it might match. And don't forget, we could only get one decent print off the victim.'

'Thanks, John. Let me know as soon as you can.' And Selby will say he gave Charles Carlos a lift on some other, unspecified, occasion which, of course, might be true. And he, Ian, had the unwelcome task of seeing Nigel Pollock once more to get his side of the episode of the victim terrorising Mrs Mostyn.

Feeling he would have more authority in a jacket and recalling that Pollock had worn one on the occasions he had seen him, Ian pulled his on and left the building having already ascertained, via a WPC posing as a potential customer, that Pollock was in his office.

It had been very late when Bruce Selby arrived back at the family home. He had asked the patrol car driver to drop him at the gates and walked up to the front door. No lights showed but the curtains were heavy and well lined. The bolts were across, he had had to knock to gain entry and woke the three remaining inhabitants.

'Bruce! Good God.' It was Maurice who opened the door, his wife and mother behind him in their dressing-gowns. 'You look bloody awful, man.' Maurice led the way into the drawing-room and poured him a measure of brandy. Bruce took it and sat down. He was pale and trembling and kept his eyes averted from the faces of his family who stood watching him.

'It was not very considerate of you not to let us know you were at least safe,' Elizabeth Selby said coldly. 'Have you spoken to the police?'

'Yes.'

'Maurice, I think I'd like a drink.' She sat in a wing-backed chair and crossed her legs, pulling the pink satin dressing-gown modestly over her knees. Norma also sat and nodded when her husband held up the bottle. 'And what exactly have you told them?'

'That I hid because I was scared. Because I didn't want to be involved and because I thought someone was trying to black-mail me and because I saw who killed him.' It came out in a rush but he did not miss the little gasp his mother made before she sipped her drink.

'This man, this homosexual, you knew him presumably?'

146

'Not very well.'

'And you saw who killed him.' It was a statement. 'And who exactly did kill him?'

'A man named Leon Dawson.'

'Ah,' she said with a note of satisfaction.

Bruce looked at her for the first time since his arrival. All his life she had exerted influence over the family, over him more than the others. As a child he had idolised her, had been so proud of her beauty when she came to sports days and cricket matches at his public school, even if she had been disappointed because he never did very well. Maurice had been the sportsman, taking after their father. His whole young existence seemed to be an endless round of trying to please her, to win her love and affection and show he was as good as Maurice, who received it without having to do anything except just be Maurice. Seeing her now, still attractive, still powerful, he tried to forget the many small hurts; the dandelions he had picked for her which she had thrown straight in the bin, the clay ornament he won at the fair which she had dropped almost immediately, an action which, although he was only seven, he believed to be deliberate. And the bigger hurts; the slaps, the withdrawal of goodnight kisses and the exclusion from whatever activities the family were involved in. But it was ingrained and at twelve thirty that September night he continued to try to please her, to tell her what she wanted to hear. Her tight smile of acknowledgement and the small nod of approval were enough to get him through the next few days.

'Where did you go, Bruce?' Norma's face was kind.

'I stayed with a friend, a woman I've known for several months.'

'Well, there you are. I said it would be some woman, didn't I? You really ought to bring your girlfriends home.' Elizabeth was pleased with him.

Bruce wondered if Carol would have anything to do with him now and he still was not sure if the police had finished with him.

'This man, Dawson did you say? I take it he's been arrested?'

'I don't know, Mother. They told me he was being questioned.'

'But they won't let him go, you saw him commit murder, didn't you?'

'I . . . yes.' I saw him hit him, Bruce admitted silently.

'And you've identified him. Is he like this Carlos man?'

'You mean gay? I think so, I'm not really sure.'

In that case, Elizabeth Selby thought, it will be Bruce's word against his, it's obvious who they'll believe. 'I think we're all tired. We can discuss it further in the morning. There's hot water, Bruce, if you want a bath.'

He did. He waited until the others had gone before pouring another drink, a large one. His mother did not approve of over-indulgence but tonight he needed it. Up to his neck in steaming water, he wondered how it would all turn out.

Carol Barnes rang in sick. Her excuse was not questioned, she had not seemed well for several days nor was she in the habit of taking time off that was not due to her. She left instructions on one or two files that needed attention and said she would probably not be off for more than twenty-four hours. She then put on her best suit, made up her face and pinned up her hair more austerely than usual and drove herself into Rickenham Green where she was to be questioned.

Before she showered she had packed Bruce's few belongings in a plastic bag and put them in the shed. He could collect them at some future time. The trees were beginning to show signs of gold and russet and the sun was warm without being over-powering yet Carol felt as if she was enveloped in a black cloud, the weight of it pressing down on her. She loved Bruce, partly perhaps, she reasoned, because he represented the child she had never had, but also because they shared so many things in common. A passionate relationship had always been out of the question, Carol was not the type, and passion soon burned out. But Bruce, she realised, did not love her, his mother's hold was too strong to allow it. She had let him stay, initially too pleased just for him to be there to question his reasons too closely, but he had not respected her wishes about going to the police and he seemed not to care about her own position. There might, she knew, be some sort of charge brought against her. If so, she would take the consequences but if it meant losing her job it was unlikely she would get another similar one.

As she walked through the revolving doors she held herself erect and decided that whatever happened she would tell the truth, she would tell them what Bruce had told her and admit that she had finally come to see that Bruce was lying.

Barry Swan left the hospital at ten thirty. Lucy was pale, her eyes blank, but she had not shed a tear. When he tried to hold her hand she had withdrawn it and turned her face away. He understood it was too soon to talk about it, but he needed some comfort himself. The doctor had said Lucy was young and healthy and that there was nothing to stop them having another baby as soon as they wanted, that the miscarriage was due simply to the fall because she was at the most vulnerable time of her pregnancy. Just like getting another dog when yours is run over, Barry thought bitterly as he drove back to the flat.

He sat at the table in the window where Lucy had first told him. There was no need to move now and the estate agents' details she had picked up on Saturday lay like an accusation in front of him. He tore them in four and took them out to the bin in the kitchen. All he could think of was what the child would have been like. And then, when he went to the bathroom, he saw his face in the mirror and self-preservation came to his rescue. He had always considered himself to be good-looking; the man that stared back at him was grey and haggard and unsmiling. What use would he be to Lucy if he didn't pull himself together? More importantly, he realised it was the first time he had dealt with a loss which really affected him. When his grandmother died he had been sad and there were still times when he missed her, but she had been over ninety and, if the doctor was to be believed, went to sleep one night and didn't wake up. No one would know if she had been aware of what was happening but she had had her time. How, then, did the families of victims feel when they were told their son or daughter had been murdered or killed in an accident, a child or adult whom they had had time to know and therefore miss more keenly?

He picked up the telephone and asked to be put through to the sister on Lucy's ward. 'Sorry to trouble you, it's Barry Swan. Look, I've decided to go into work. I can be reached there if I'm needed.' He gave the number and hung up.

10

Ian returned from Nigel Pollock's offices to find Doc Harris on his way out. 'You've got a right one there,' he commented.

'What?'

'In the cells. Now she's been charged it seems she's developed asthma, brought on, she claims, by being confined. Nothing wrong with her that won't be cured with a good sleep and a couple of aspirins. Still drunk from last night. You're not listening, are you?'

'Sorry. No. Things on my mind.' And Mark and Lara to contend with later.

'Work?'

'Yes. And a certain young lady.'

'Lucky old you.'

'Mark's latest. Difficult girl to talk to.'

'Well, take them all out to eat, it'll break the ice and give your lovely wife a rest. And Ian . . .'

'Yes?'

'Take it easy or you'll end up in my surgery.'

'I will.' He smiled and watched the Doc amble towards the exit. Nothing and no one would make that man hurry.

He waited until DC Gibbons had shown Carol Barnes out then asked how it went.

'She's a very straightforward lady. She didn't say so in so many words, but she's more than fond of Selby and he's let her down. To summarise, sir, she took him in believing it was to become a permanent arrangement then he implied Pollock was trying to twist his arm over some planning application, not on her side but to do with something more major. Next thing is she hears the gossip and reads the *Herald* and realises there's a lot more to it than that. She's holding her hand up to sheltering him but she now thinks he's lying about everything.'

They were, without realising it, both heading towards the canteen. As soon as they were at basement level they could smell bacon and fried onions and Ian envied those officers who could eat rolls and butties mid-morning as well as proper meals and not gain weight. They purchased two coffees at the counter and took them to a table.

'What was he lying about specifically?'

Brenda tucked her hair behind her ears and shrugged. 'She says she doesn't know, just that he is. He gave her the same story we got.'

'About Dawson and the photograph.'

'Yes. But without naming Dawson.'

'Does she think he might have done it?'

'She says she's had time to think about it and she believes not. That he would be more of a mess than he is if he had. She was very matter of fact about her own position.' Brenda picked up her mug in both hands and took a sip of milky coffee. 'I feel sorry for her.'

'Oh?'

'She's not the sort to attract sympathy, she's too self-assured and professional, but she's hurting all right, and worried about her future. I mean, she's possibly been hiding a murderer. Anyway, what did Pollock have to say?'

'As I thought, Carlos had been bragging about helping him out, going around saying he'd get the old woman out for him. Pollock claims he warned him off, threatened him, in fact, saying that wasn't the way he operated and if he didn't cut it out he'd come to us. It confirms Dawson's story, he also said Carlos was always boasting and that he wasn't even certain he was responsible for the vandalism. Oh, did Markham tell you we got the gen from Bristol?' Brenda shook her head and the long hair fell forward again. 'The two lads who came to see Carlos, they're

152

clean.' Markham had also checked with the woman with whom they were staying, who was a cousin of one of them. They had not had enough money for hotels or guest houses so their holiday consisted of spending a few days here and there with relatives. Charles Carlos was an acquaintance rather than a friend but they thought they might as well look him up as they were in the area. It was unlikely they were suspects but as the time of death would never be pinpointed no one could produce a perfect alibi. For the moment their names would remain on the file.

'Where do we go from here?' Brenda asked, echoing Ian's own thoughts.

'We start again,' he answered with some determination. 'Back to square one.'

'Which is where?'

'The disappearance of Bruce Selby. Fancy a ride out to Maple Grove?'

'Why not, it's a nice day.' The smile was a flash of white teeth, open and friendly. If only Lara were more like that, Ian thought, amazed that one thin student could cause so much anxiety in the Roper household.

Elizabeth Selby had slept well despite being aware that Bruce's having taken himself to the police station did not mean it was the end of the matter. Brenda noticed the difference immediately. Mrs Selby was dressed in expensive navy slacks and a long-sleeved shirt. Around her neck was a thick, gold chain and she had painted her nails pearly pink. 'Good morning.' She greeted them cheerfully and offered them coffee. 'We can sit outside, the weather's perfect.' The blue-striped umbrella had been removed but the rest of the garden furniture remained. The woman who helped out brought the tray and nodded an acknowledgement to Brenda whom she had seen previously. She had seemed to know little of the habits of the Selby family other than those of Elizabeth with whom she came into daily contact. To her, Bruce, like all men, was someone who came and went and did not interfere with the running of a house.

'Smells good.'

'Thank you, sir.'

Some sort of casserole was being cooked, a rich beef and garlic and red wine concoction, Ian thought. His stomach rumbled.

Mrs Selby poured coffee, having dismissed the woman with a small nod of her head. 'We're having a few friends over for lunch, I hope this won't take too long.'

'Killing the fatted calf?'

'Pardon?'

Ian had spoken softly. 'Nothing. It must be a tremendous relief to you, knowing your son's safe.'

'I can't tell you how pleased we were to see him last night. I rang everyone this morning, people have been so kind and understanding. I don't know how I'd have coped if anything had happened to him. Bruce was a fool, Chief Inspector, I told him so in no uncertain terms, but as you're aware, he's completely innocent, his only crime is lack of moral fibre. God knows we tried to instil some into him. Anyway, starting with this little lunch we're putting it all behind us. I believe you've arrested someone?'

'No.'

'No? But my son explained, he saw whoever did it. Surely you don't think he'd make something like that up?'

'He saw someone hit the victim.'

'This really is too much. We haven't had a minute's peace for ages.' Her hand shook as she replaced the bone china cup on its saucer. 'Are we to be subjected to more questioning?'

'Where is your son?'

'Upstairs. He's attending to some paperwork. Must I disturb him, he's been through enough already?'

'No, no need. And Maurice and Norma?'

'They have both gone to work. The children are still with friends, we thought it was the least we could do for Bruce, to allow him one day without them under his feet. Still, they'll be back at school in a couple of days.'

'This is good coffee.'

'Thank you.' She looked up in surprise and returned Ian's smile.

It did not, he thought, take much to put her at ease and she was very much a woman used to having her own way. A strong, autocratic woman, one who would mould her family to fit her idea of how they should be, one who was used to being obeyed and who probably thought the police were a load of clod-hoppers, tolerated in her home only because she had no choice. 'I'm sorry we've had to trouble you again, Mrs Selby, Constable Gibbons and I will leave you to enjoy your lunch party.' Before pulling out a notebook he saw the fleeting puzzled expression in her face. They had, after all, not asked any questions. 'It was seven forty-five when Councillor Jenkins rang you? The night Bruce disappeared, that is?'

'The night? Good heavens, it seems a lifetime ago. Yes. If that's what I said at the time it must have been. Why?'

'Just checking. There's no problem, he confirmed it.' Ian smiled pleasantly. Let her make of that what she would. He hesitated in the doorway. 'Oh, one other thing. You'll recall my mentioning having been here on another occasion.'

'Yes.' The retort came from between stiff lips. Elizabeth Selby stood, as she must have done many times when she wanted to intimidate her family.

'It came back to me. Theo Selby. We were investigating some rather unpleasant rumours concerning young boys who had been approached by a man – approached, as I remember, for the purpose of sexual favours.'

'How dare you. My husband was completely vindicated at the time. Rumours were exactly what they were. Your insinuations are beyond the pale. You can leave now but this is not the last of it, I shall be making a formal complaint.'

'We'll be in touch,' was Ian's enigmatic response.

'You're on to something, aren't you?' Brenda inquired when they were in the car.

'I think so.' He refused to be drawn further except to say, 'But I believe we'll leave it to Markham.' Yes, Markham, he thought as Brenda started the engine, with his menacing manner and total disregard for wealth, position and finer feelings. There was a strong possibility Markham might just succeed.

'It's no skin off my nose.' It was a typical Markham comment which followed the Chief's instructions and the warning that Mrs Selby would not hesitate to go through official channels if he didn't play it by the book. Markham had been on the receiving end of disciplinary action before and had, so far, come through unscathed. 'Now, sir?'

'No, wait until this evening, when they're all at home.'

Markham shrugged, his curiosity unaroused, although he realised he was being left to form his own conclusions.

'Make sure you take someone with you.' It was a safeguard; in Markham's case it was always better to have a witness.

Layer upon layer of grey cloud was building up on the horizon as Ian pulled out of the car-park. He noticed that whoever was responsible for the raised flower beds had been busy. The tired and dying bedding plants had been removed, the earth was now bare and neatly forked and had been covered with what looked like wood chippings. There were trails of mud leading around the side of the station house. The roses, at the far side of the parking area, were still in bloom but their turn would come. He thought there was nothing more depressing than a bed of hard-pruned roses.

The rush-hour traffic had slackened. In the High Street were several illegally parked cars and a few small queues remained at the bus-stops as an early evening calm settled over Rickenham Green. He stopped for cigarettes then carried on to Belmont Terrace. The Fiesta, although he was supposed to share it with Moira, had now become known as Mark's and was parked outside the house in what was usually Ian's place. He felt a small surge of annoyance. It was not a good omen and he tried to quell it. Deep down he knew it was because he was impatient to learn what Markham had achieved but there was the added irritation of Lara's presence. He should feel flattered, not resentful, that his son chose to bring his girlfriend home. Twenty yards on he indicated and pulled into a neighbour's space. It was illogical how possessive they all were. It was a public highway and there were no parking restrictions. 'Which, as we all know,' he muttered, 'means absolutely anyone can park where they damned well like.'

'Moira?' The house was unnaturally quiet.

'Out here.'

She was making tea in the kitchen. 'Where are they?'

'Upstairs, unpacking. They were here when I got back from work.'

He kissed her absent-mindedly. 'Have you done any food?'

'Ian, I only walked through the door ten minutes ago.'

It was definitely not a good omen, he thought, if he had his wife to contend with as well. He wondered why he had bothered to make the effort to get home early. And then he remembered all the times he had not. 'I'm sorry. I thought, as it's their first night, we could go out to eat. You know, break the ice a bit?' He did not mention it was the Doc's idea.

'Great.' She had been hoping he would suggest it. 'They'll be down in a minute.'

By the time four mugs of tea were on the table Mark and Lara appeared. 'Hi, Dad.' To Ian's amazement, his son shook his hand.

'Good to see you. And you, Lara.'

'Hello.'

Ian glanced at Moira and widened his eyes as if to say, oh well. She grinned in response. 'I thought, if you'd like to, we'd go out for a meal.'

'Indian,' Mark said immediately. Like his father, he would eat it several times a week, given the choice. Yet it had taken Moira ages to persuade Ian to try it many years ago.

'Lara?'

'I don't mind.'

'Good, the Taj Mahal it is then.' And please God she takes that sullen expression off her face before I'm tempted to do it for her, he added silently.

By tacit agreement between the senior Ropers they went out early, stopping for a couple of drinks in the Crown first. Ian introduced Lara to the landlord and a couple of regulars who knew Mark. He wondered what they made of her with the chunky jewellery, the mass of hair and the black leggings, cut off at the ankle, the sort of short dress thing she wore over them and what, to him, could only be described as hob-nail boots. However, it was her manners which troubled him more. She made no effort to converse or even answer some of the inquiries made of her as to her future and student life. It might be a bore, being asked the same old thing by people who had long since made their choices, but he still considered it rude not to humour them.

The proprietor of the Indian restaurant fussed over them in his usual way but left them alone when the food arrived. Mark soon cleared his plate and began to help himself to what Lara had been pushing around hers. 'I could eat it all again,' he said when they had finished. 'It was lovely, wasn't it, Lara? Thanks, Dad.'

Lara, hair falling forward and hiding her small face, stared at the hot-plates. Mark shrugged and even in the dim lighting his parents noticed the faint flush of his cheeks. With Mark it signified anger, not embarrassment.

'Have you finished, Lara?' It was Moira who asked as the waiter hovered, ready to clear the table.

'Yes, thanks.'

They walked home in silence, each deep in thought.

'There's something wrong with that girl,' Ian told Moira as he pulled his tie to one side to loosen it before undressing for bed. 'And I'll tell you one thing, if she doesn't buck up her ideas I'm going to say something, whatever Mark might think. Why don't you have a word with him, see if you can find out what's wrong. I can't believe she's simply that shy.'

'It might be better coming from you.'

'No, he's always been closer to you.' Ian regretted this was so.

'Once, when he was a boy. He's more likely to talk to you now.'

'Do you think so?' He was pleased. 'I'll see what I can do tomorrow.'

If anyone had been surprised to see DS Barry Swan arrive during the middle of the morning, no one said so. His face was grim and he barely spoke. He volunteered to reinterview Martin Cook who was not due at the Stag and Hounds until the evening shift. Barry, in his bitter frame of mind, found it pathetic to hear a grown man talking about missing his boyfriend, but was determined not to allow his personal problems to influence his professional ones.

At the end of the interview Barry had typed up the report himself, left it with the control room and read through what he had missed the previous day. There had been no phone call from the hospital. At five o'clock he left and went back to see Lucy.

'I don't know,' he told Ian the following morning when he asked how she was taking it. 'She won't speak to me.' Ian knew the feeling. 'I've tried but she's just shutting me out. I don't know what I can do.'

'Keep trying. It's trite, I know, but time will do the rest. Come on, Elizabeth Selby's downstairs.'

Elizabeth Selby was indeed downstairs, along with her solicitor, although if she was here only to make a complaint Ian did not see the necessity of his presence. They had been asked to wait in an interview room rather than an office. This was deliberate policy on Ian's part.

Markham had succeeded. He had penetrated the veneer, needled the woman to such an extent that she had lost her temper. Ian hoped the complaint was being made due to loss of face rather than for genuine reasons. He had, he now saw, been subconsciously piecing it together even when he believed his mind was not working. And now it was make or break.

'Good morning, Mrs Selby. I didn't expect to see you again quite so soon.' He kept his tone and expression formally bland.

'I think the time for pleasantries is over. This is John Bradcock, my solicitor. You obviously know I'm here to voice my complaints. You and your officers have done nothing more than harass my family which is despicable under the circumstances. We have willingly given all the information you've required in order to be able to trace my son. He's home now, thank God, but you won't let it rest. Last night, just as we were beginning to relax, you send two of your thugs over. That sergeant was particularly offensive, frankly I'm amazed you employ such people.' She paused for breath.

'You are quite free to make any complaint you wish, Mrs Selby, but you are wasting police time demanding to speak to a senior officer in order to do so. I understand the desk sergeant explained the procedure to you quite adequately. However, as you are here, and with Mr Bradcock in attendance, we might as well use the opportunity to clear up a couple of matters which have been bothering us.'

'I really don't think –'

'Mrs Selby.' John Bradcock placed a hand on her arm. 'The police have a job to do, obstructing them will not help. I suggest you answer their questions then we will do as the desk sergeant recommended.' He had already tried to persuade her this was the right course.

'Very well, if I must.' John had been their solicitor for years and Theo had always claimed he was one of the best. It was probably wisest to go along with what he said. There was too much at stake to do otherwise.

Barry pulled up a chair. He and Ian faced Elizabeth Selby and her solicitor across the table; Bradcock, he noticed, sat slightly back and to one side of his client. He was therefore not the sort to interfere, to refuse to allow her to answer at every opportunity.

'Mrs Selby, you have been questioned in your own home on

several occasions, but as you are now here, I would like to make this a formal interview and record our conversation. Do you have any objections?'

'I . . .' She glanced at Bradcock who shook his head. 'No.'

Ian switched on the recording machine and noted the date and time and the names of those present, double-checking that she was fully aware of what was happening.

'I'm not a fool,' she snapped.

'I would like to start with the night your son, Bruce Selby, disappeared. You say he did not return home on the Wednesday night. Had you any idea where he was?'

'None. He has since told me he spent the night with a woman named Carol Barnes.'

This had been confirmed by both Bruce and Carol.

'But you weren't unduly worried.'

'No. There have been other occasions when he stayed away.'

'On those occasions he usually let you know.'

'Yes.'

'And on Thursday, after you received a call from Councillor Jenkins to say he had not turned up for the meeting, you still weren't too concerned. Let me put it this way, it wasn't until Friday that you contacted us.'

'Bruce is a middle-aged man, Chief Inspector. I have already told you, I didn't think anyone would take a lot of notice. I was, initially, impressed with the way you dealt with the situation, I did not expect you to take me seriously.'

She had a point. 'Mrs Selby, I have not yet had a chance to study DS Markham's report concerning his visit to your home last evening, therefore you must forgive me if my questions are repetitive.' He had studied it, of course, gone over it three or four times, in fact. And Markham was as certain as he was becoming himself. Briefly Ian went over what Bruce had told them regarding Pollock and Charles Carlos and Leon Dawson. 'And your son still claims he saw Mr Carlos being murdered.'

'But you, for some inexplicable reason, won't believe him.'

'I do believe him.'

'Then what –'

'He did see Leon Dawson hit the victim, but he also saw who killed him.'

'I really don't understand what you're getting at.'

'Excuse me for one moment.' Ian left the room but only to confirm something. 'Mrs Selby, your son is also here. He's ready to make a new statement.'

'Bruce didn't do it.' She was scornful. 'He isn't capable of tying his own shoe laces.'

'On the Thursday night,' Ian continued, ignoring her outburst, 'you received that telephone call. It was seven forty-five, or thereabouts. Bruce is conscientious, he would not miss a council meeting unless something unavoidable or really important turned up. Now, I've been thinking long and hard about this. From what we know of your son he has few hobbies – his boat, yes, but nothing else. Forgive me for saying so, but you yourself admitted he is boring. His circle of acquaintances is limited and there have been so few women over the years it's hardly worth mentioning them. Until he met Carol Barnes the ones he did see were unavailable; married, confessed spinsters or females who, like Bruce, enjoyed the odd meal out in mixed company. Carol Barnes was different.'

'Yes. Obviously. They were virtually living together.'

'And you, for whatever reasons, did not like the idea that Miss Barnes and Bruce might become a permanent couple.'

'Good heavens, no.' She laughed nervously. 'It wasn't that.'

'What was it then? Did you know, perhaps, that it could never happen, that Bruce would not be able to keep up the façade?'

'What are you implying, Chief Inspector?'

'That your son is homosexual, that he has tried to prove, perhaps both to himself and to you, that it is not so – hence the women who were really no danger to his remaining single – and that he was, justifiably, if your expressed views are to be believed, terrified of you finding out. Carol Barnes was the answer. They were companionable, enjoyed the same things and

162

did not expect much out of life. They could marry, you'd be happy, they would have some sort of a life together, but, more importantly, Bruce could carry on as he was before.' Elizabeth Selby clamped her lips together. 'The loser is Miss Barnes, she genuinely loved your son.'

'How dare you insinuate such a thing. That lout, that sergeant who came last night, suggested the same thing. My family is not like that. I shall sue you for defamation.'

'But Bruce admitted someone took his photograph with the victim's arm around his shoulder.'

'It was a foolish prank. Anyway, where is this supposed photograph?'

Leon Dawson had burned it, but he was not about to tell her so. 'We have proof that Charles Carlos was in your son's car. He is, as I said, making a new statement at this moment. The victim had had sexual relations sometime during the day of his murder. Tests are now conclusive enough to show who with. Bruce has agreed for us to take samples and that will –'

'He didn't. My son did *not* have sex with him. He –' She stopped, her eyes in her white face were enormous. 'May I have a drink of water, please?'

'We had better start again, Mrs Selby. This time it might be wiser if you told us exactly how it was.'

'I'm shattered,' Barry said when the interview was over. 'And I wasn't asking the questions.'

But it took your mind off things for a while, Ian thought, and I'm glad. 'Me too. Think of the time we've wasted. Come on, let's go for a pint.' It was, he supposed, partly his own fault, his dogmatic refusal to believe in coincidence. Pollock, Dawson, Patti Evans, Carol Barnes, Selby and the victim himself were all connected but by work or emotional ties. He had not been able to see the wood for the trees, he thought as, to humour Barry, they made their way to the Feathers. Drained of energy, he found it difficult to comprehend that the people they passed in

163

the street were going about their ordinary business, that their lives, hopefully, were not touched by murder.

Ian ordered a pint of Guinness as there was no real ale, and Barry had a light ale. 'Nothing for me,' he said when Ian offered to buy him some lunch. And then, after a silence, 'Lucy's coming home tomorrow.'

'Give it time, Barry, just let her know you're with her, it'll be all right.' Ian sipped the drink; another pint and he would not feel like eating. It was hard to feel in a celebratory mood knowing what Barry was going through; but although the pieces had not been tidied up, there was no longer any doubt.

Bruce Selby had told his mother he had started visiting the Pink Elephant, assuming that she did not know what sort of clientele it was aimed at. Even if she did know, he could use the excuse that it was Pollock he went there to see. She had met Nigel and admired him for making his way in the world although he would never be totally acceptable because it was through business that he had succeeded. When she learned of his new acquaintances her fears were confirmed. To her Bruce had always been a lame duck, she had never been able to bring herself to love him and she found his attempts to win her love irritating and ridiculous. Like Ian, she suspected that one reason Bruce might not have turned up at the council meeting was because he had found an opportunity to indulge what she called his perversion. When she saw what was happening she had to prevent not only the act but the scandal that might befall her family. Because of her own views she was unable to see that others might think differently, that many of her circle of friends would wonder what she was making a fuss about. Right up to the end Bruce had tried to protect her and Ian thought it was the saddest thing that his mother thought less of him for doing so.

'What made you suspect it was Mrs Selby?'

'Several things in the end.' Ian wiped Guinness froth from his top lip with the back of his hand.

'Is it a secret or am I allowed to know?'

'Brenda suspected that Mrs Selby's views on homosexuality

were over the top, that there had to be a reason for her reactionary stand. And don't forget, the sister-in-law thought Bruce might be asexual. And although he patronised the Elephant, we overlooked the fact that he did so to be amongst his own kind.'

'But he wasn't overt, not according to the rest of the customers.'

'No, he didn't dare to be in case it got back to his mother. None of the suspects had a concrete alibi, understandably as we didn't know ourselves exactly when Carlos was killed. But it was puzzling that no one tried to establish one.'

'You mean because *they* didn't know when he was killed either.'

'Precisely. But we were sidetracked by the many connections between the suspects, forgetting that the one person who might know exactly where Bruce was on that Thursday evening, and who also had a method of transport, was his mother. Once she received that call from the Town Hall she put two and two together. She's a fit woman for her age and she plays golf regularly. It wouldn't have taken much strength to wield that iron, and couple that with anger . . .' There was no need to expound. Bruce had confirmed that his mother had hit Carlos three times, the first blow coming from behind when he had no chance of defending himself and, engaged as he was, he would not have heard her approach.

'I know all this, Ian. I was there at the interview. But I still don't see how you were so sure.'

'It was Mark.'

'Mark?'

'My son.' He could have bitten off his tongue. The last thing Barry needed was a reminder of his own progeny. He carried on quickly. 'This latest girlfriend. She's a pain, to be honest. She's sullen and rude and it's not the usual adolescent thing, she's twenty. She's affecting the atmosphere at home and I wondered how I'd feel if Mark decided his future lay with her.'

'Ah. You wondered how far you'd go to prevent that.'

'Yes. I wouldn't resort to murder of course, and I know it's

165

none of my business if they make each other happy. What he does is his own affair although I won't be subjected to that sort of rudeness in my own home. But I'm not Mrs Selby, a woman who has managed to keep both her sons under her roof all their lives. It works with Maurice and Norma and they've done their bit by producing a son to carry on the Selby name. Elizabeth Selby's terrified of scandal, I believe she couldn't have coped with a second lot, not after what her husband was alleged to have done. Nothing ever came of it but I think she knew. I think other people knew as well. She was not about to go through something similar with Bruce.'

Barry looked at his glass and was surprised to find it empty. 'Shall we have another one?' Ian nodded. 'I'm glad I didn't have to witness Bruce's interview,' he said when he returned to the table. Markham and DC Gibbons had been responsible for that. 'Blubbering into his handkerchief, was how Markham put it, because he couldn't save his precious mother. And after all she'd put him through.'

'He adored her. It was as simple as that.' Brenda, Ian knew, had been more sympathetic. Bruce Selby had described the incident in the Pink Elephant when Carlos had put his arm around him. 'I felt so ashamed, I enjoyed it, you see,' he had said. And then he had gone out to the lavatory prior to leaving for the council meeting, although he was a little late. There in the back alley he had seen Leon Dawson hit Carlos who had fallen to the ground. Before he was on his feet Dawson strode off. Carlos had staggered out into the main road and when Bruce got into his car he saw him.

'I stopped to offer him a lift,' he said. 'He was hurt, not badly, but enough, and shaken. He put his hand on my knee and I, well, I knew I wasn't going to make that meeting. We drove down to the river, I couldn't risk being seen parked in the car. Chaz went on ahead while I parked in the High Street and followed him. And then, well . . . he was . . . well, the next thing I knew he was on the ground and my mother was standing there with a golf club in her hand. She hit him again, twice.' Bruce had started to cry at that point. 'He was dead, I've never seen anyone dead

166

before, but I knew it. She didn't seem to care. She didn't even speak to me except tell me to help her drag the body under some bushes. "Go to your meeting," she told me. "Make some excuse about the car breaking down or something, we'll discuss it later." I couldn't believe it, I just could not believe how cold she was about it all. I didn't go, I couldn't, and I couldn't go home either. What will happen to her?'

Neither Markham nor Brenda would say. Knowing what they did of Elizabeth Selby it would be highly unlikely she would be tried on the grounds of diminished responsibility and even if a lawyer thought they could get away with it, Mrs Selby would not allow herself to be thought of in those terms.

Ian went up for more drinks and Barry suddenly realised he had paid for two rounds. 'I couldn't resist it, I've ordered a slice of their steak and kidney. Are you sure you don't want anything?'

'Perhaps a sandwich.'

'It's OK, I'll get it.'

Barry smiled, feeling a slight tightness around his mouth where tension had done its work. Food and drink, the Chief's way of offering sympathy.

They sat and ate in silence, Barry more hungry than he had thought. What sort of woman was it who went to look for her son, a grown man, in the pub, and with what intentions? Had she merely gone there with the idea of making her presence felt, to show him that she knew what was going on and try to put a stop to it before things went a stage further? It was likely Selby would have responded to his mother's wishes if she had arrived ten minutes sooner. Immediately she had received the call from Councillor Jenkins she had guessed where Bruce was to be found and left the house at once, arriving at the pub just as Bruce was getting into his car. Imagining she was wrong, that he was going to the meeting, she had not wanted him to see her so had waited until he drove off. But Bruce had slowed down and she had seen Carlos get into the passenger seat.

'Bruce didn't see me,' she had admitted. 'He had other things on his mind. I followed them. I saw where they went. I cannot begin to describe the scene, and I will not attempt to do so. Suffice it to say that it was made easy for me because that man, Carlos, was standing and my son was not.'

Mrs Selby's car had been inspected. Her golf clubs were in the boot. There was no question her actions were premeditated: she had gone armed with one of them, and a couple of golf balls in case she was seen. The grass near the bridge was short, suitable to serve as a practice area.

When Ian and Barry arrived back at the station there was a message from Lucy. She was at home, having discharged herself from hospital.

PC Mallet informed Mrs Mostyn that, in all likelihood, Charles Carlos had been responsible for her problems. In time, if there were no further incidents, they would be certain of it.

'Was it you or that detective who sorted it out?' she asked.

'A bit of both, I suppose.' He had, after all, reported Mr Gilbert's observations and Markham had somehow incorporated them into the murder inquiry. However, as far as Mrs Mostyn was concerned, she could sleep at nights without half listening for footsteps in the street.

It was pleasantly warm, he was back in shirt-sleeves again and a cup of tea would not come amiss. No chance here, but Bert Gilbert would oblige. He made his old-fashioned gesture of parting, two fingers touching the brim of his helmet, and crossed the road. Mr Gilbert was out but he came across him later, down by the old railway tracks, seated on a canvas folding chair, sketching the weeds and wild flowers to which he would later add his water-colours. An idea came to PC Mallet. 'Bert, would you sell me one of your paintings?'

'Sell you one? Whatever do you want with one of my ham-fisted efforts? I'll give you one if you like.'

'No, I insist. They're good, you know. I'd like one for my living-room wall.'

Bert Gilbert shook his head. 'As you wish.' But a few extra bob would mean an extra night or two down at the Legion.

'How about if I come round later, when I'm off duty?'

'Yes.' His face lit up at the thought of some evening company. 'We could pop down the Club if you like, after. They're not all old like me, there's one or two quite likely females.'

PC Mallet grinned. He knew Bert thought it was time he was married. 'We'll do that. Seven thirty all right?' He carried on his solitary patrolling, pleased he had made someone's day. And you never know, he thought, the paintings are good, might even be worth something one day. Not that he intended parting with it.

Moira had called in at Deirdre's when she finished work with the idea of leaving the coast clear for Ian to speak to Mark or both of them. They had been asleep when she and Ian left for work and it was nice to have breakfast without trying to make conversation with Lara. Deirdre insisted that it was the time of day for sherry or gin, not tea, and it was after seven before Moira got home. The house was ominously silent. She hoped Ian hadn't gone too far, the youngsters departed and himself in the pub cooling his heels. Fifteen minutes later as she was making some chilli, enough for four, but half of which could be frozen if her fears were correct, she heard a key in the lock. Ian's shoulders were drooped and he looked utterly drained.

'How did it go?'

'We've got her.' He sat at the kitchen table, too tired to move.

Moira frowned, misunderstanding him because she assumed he was referring to Lara.

'His mother. He was trying to protect her.'

The murder. Of course. He had not spoken to Mark then. Perhaps it was best, in his present frame of mind he might have said more than he meant.

'She hasn't admitted it in so many words, but she's not denying it either, and the son witnessed it.' Hopefully Forensics would come up with a blood group match on one of the golf

169

clubs. Elizabeth Selby may have tried to wash it off but it would not be so easy if it had splashed on to the leather binding around the handle. He wondered what sort of life it had been for Bruce, so very much under his mother's aegis, and what he would make of his new-found freedom. Perhaps, at last, he would use it to be himself, the person he had denied for so many years. Time would tell, first he had to face a possible sentence for his part in shielding a murderer. Murderess, he corrected himself.

'Have you seen Mark?' He remembered what he was supposed to do.

'No, and he hasn't left a note either. I don't know if they'll want feeding or not.'

Moira was annoyed, but, in his view, with reason. Common politeness dictated he should do so, especially as Moira was at work all day. He realised that Elizabeth Selby must often have felt the same, but she had taken things to extremes. They had just sat down to eat when Mark and Lara returned from a five o'clock performance at the cinema.

'Smells great,' Mark said.

'You'll have to wait or do your own rice. I'm not going to let mine get cold.'

'Bad day at the office, Mother?' He grinned and patted her on the head.

'No, I just wish you'd let me know, that's all. You might've gone for a pizza or something.'

'I left a note.' His voice rose slightly, in the accusatory fashion of one who is innocent.

'What note? I didn't see one.'

'I put it in the usual place, by the kettle.' The Ropers had always done this because it was the first object to be used when they walked into the house.

'Well, it certainly wasn't there.'

'I put it there, you saw me, didn't you, Lara?'

Lara's hair, hanging forward, did not disguise the redness that was creeping over her natural pallor.

'Lara?'

170

She did not look up. Mark went over to her. 'Did you move it?'

'You're twenty, you're a free agent, you don't need to leave notes.' It was the longest sentence she had spoken but Moira and Ian were more amazed at the content.

'I do. You wouldn't like it if you had to cook and you didn't know if your guests were hungry or even what time they'd be back.'

'I want to go home,' she said defiantly. And with that she left the room and ran noisily up the stairs. Five minutes later she returned, carrying her hold-all, and from the silence in the kitchen she knew they had been talking about her. 'Where's the station?'

'Look, Lara,' Ian began, 'there's no need for you to go, can't we discuss whatever's bothering –'

'No. I'm going home.'

'Mark?' Ian looked inquiringly at his son.

'She must do whatever she wants. She's a free agent, after all,' he said, sarcastically echoing her own words.

'All right. I'll run you to the station, but you're coming back if there aren't any suitable connections. Where're you intending to go?'

'To my mother's in London.'

Mark opened his mouth to speak then changed his mind.

Lara didn't speak until they reached the station. There were a few other passengers waiting for the train to Ipswich and from there she would be able to get a connection to London. 'Thanks,' she said, taking the bag from him. 'There's no need to wait, I'll be fine.'

He watched as she walked along the platform until she was out of sight behind the closed tea bar. She was a pathetic figure, so small and thin and unable to find happiness. Now all he had to do was face Mark.

Mark, with the resilience of youth, was scraping the last of the chilli and rice from his plate. 'Sorry about that,' he said. 'I knew things weren't working out, but I didn't realise it was that bad.'

171

'Want to tell me about it? Over a pint?'

'If you're paying. I'm skint.' When wasn't he?

'So,' Ian said when Mark had gone to his room. 'There's no mother in London. I hope she'll be all right. Rotten background, from what Mark told me, and it seems she couldn't cope with us, she thought we were too cloying, too much the perfect family. She said that, apparently, "You and your bloody perfect parents." '

'Us?' Moira laughed. 'It must've been bad if that's what she thinks.'

'Mark knew and thought he could make it up to her. It's not, it seems, what she wants. Anyway, he reassured me he had a feeling she wanted to break it off even before they arrived. Better here, he can start the new term afresh. Shouldn't be too difficult, they'll both be surrounded by other students.' But deep down he was pleased and he felt ashamed for feeling so at someone else's expense. Mark would learn that, like Ian, he would only be able to marry, or live with, someone he loved, not someone who attracted his pity. Ian would never know that Mark cried that night.

'Lucy, shouldn't you be resting?'

She was in the kitchen, making a salad because that was all she could find in the fridge. 'What for? I'm not pregnant now. I don't want to be fussed over, I just want to forget it. You might as well open some wine, it can't do me any harm now.'

How long would the bitterness last? he wondered. It was no one's fault, it was a pure accident and it might be that fate had decided the time was not right. The strap of Lucy's shoulder bag had caught over the knob of the banister and, being extra careful because of her condition, she had tried to regain her balance in a way she might not have done otherwise. She was right, they had to try to put it behind them.

In bed he gently put an arm around her, to comfort her, no more than that. She removed it. 'Don't,' she said.

He lay on his back staring at the ceiling for a long time, knowing Lucy was also awake. It was going to be a long and difficult haul back to normality and he wondered if either of them had the strength for it. But time, as Ian had pointed out, would tell.

Half-way through that final interview Elizabeth Selby had known she would be arrested; she had suspected it the previous day, when they had sent the uncouth DS Markham to see her. She knew she could not bear the shame that would fall on her family, the shame for which she was now responsible in trying to avert a different sort. She had tried to bluff it out using the excuse of a complaint, attack being the best form of defence. She had failed. There might be like-minded people out there who believed she had done the right thing, but there would not be many, there would be no female pressure groups trying to save her. Prison could just about be faced, although it was not how she had imagined ending her days, the shame could not. When it was over it would all come out, the newspapers would have a field day resurrecting that little peccadillo of Theo's. He had been a good and loving husband and an excellent father and although they had had two sons, his behaviour was never less than proper as far as they were concerned. She had never got over him being caught exposing himself to a schoolboy. It might have been the only time, she never asked and it was never discussed. Certainly he was never caught again. That was many years ago, when she was in her twenties. Bruce was like Theo, in looks and temperament, and maybe that was why she was never able to treat him as she did Maurice, why she would not allow herself to become close to him. Terrified he might go the same way, her fears exaggerated when, after three years at university, he had not brought a girl home or even mentioned one, she tightened her rein. Bruce, she supposed, had not brought Carol Barnes home in case she voiced her suspicions or belittled him in front of her. She was quite capable of doing so. And he had become more furtive, not telling her exactly where he had been. She had had to know.

In her handbag was a bottle of strong painkillers for the shoulder trouble she had been experiencing recently. The bag had lain on the table in the interview room and when they brought her tea she was tempted to swallow the lot. However, it could not be done without them noticing and preventing her, or pumping her stomach out if she did succeed. Later, they had searched her bag and taken it away, saying she would be given the prescribed dose as and when it was needed.

Sitting on the edge of her uncomfortable bed in the cell she smiled wryly. How much more convenient for everyone if she had done so. An easy way out for her and it would have saved the taxpayers a large amount of money. However, John Bradcock would find her a good barrister, money could do that, at least. She toyed with ideas, possible defence arguments, extenuating circumstances. Only later, when she had eaten a meal not as bad as she feared it might be, did she realise there were none. She might as well plead guilty and get it over with quickly. Tomorrow she would ask John, but she had a feeling that if she did so there would not be the necessity of a public trial.

After a couple of days Mark perked up and Moira was glad to see the dark shadows under his eyes had disappeared. Feeling relief that both husband and son were back on an even keel, she handed him a ten pound note and told him to go and buy himself some CDs or something. They had not spoiled him, had gone out of their way not to do so, aware of the dangers of having only one child. His mouth dropped open. 'It must be the menopause,' Mark said as he pocketed the money in case she changed her mind.

She would, she decided, call in and see Lucy Swan even though Barry had told Ian she did not want any visitors. Lucy's depression was genuine, but more easily dealt with than her own family at times. As she watched Mark's lanky shape wandering off towards the shops she spared a thought for Elizabeth Selby and decided that, although she could not possibly condone what she had done, she could understand it.

Carol Barnes went back to work and awaited her fate stoically. Maybe one day she would meet another man with whom she wanted to share her life; if not, she would content herself with the small things she already enjoyed. If she knew Bruce, whatever his feelings for her he would not want the constant reminder that it was with her he had stayed knowing his mother had committed a murder. She allowed herself to believe he had loved her during the short time they had had together.

Ian and Moira decided they would repeat the experience and go back to Falmouth at the same time as Mark. It was Moira's idea but her motives were two-fold. Before they set off she announced that only one car was necessary, the Fiesta, because with winter in the offing, she might like to use it more often herself. Mark grumbled for most of the journey but finally admitted he didn't really need it. Everything he wanted was within walking distance; Cornwall was not without its share of public transport and Truro was easily reached by train.

They did not see Lara during the weekend, and both refrained from mentioning her.

Ian, driving a car smaller than the one he was used to, thought it fitting, as they returned, that they had spent the weekend away. It had started from there really, returning to find Brenda investigating Bruce's disappearance, and now it was over. And Elizabeth Selby, to give her her due, had finally made an unequivocal statement.

'I know what you're thinking,' Moira said as they neared Rickenham Green.

'Oh?'

'That as it's already nine o'clock, you might as well park on the

Green, convenient for a couple of drinks, and then we can finish the evening off in the Taj Mahal.'

'Not bad. But who said anything about finishing the evening off at that point? We'll have the house to ourselves again.'

'Ian!' She slapped his thigh, but she was smiling.

There was, Ian realised as he dipped a piece of nan bread into a rather brightly coloured massala sauce, one aspect of the case which had not been cleared up: where Charles Carlos got the extra money. Martin Cook had hinted that there might be other men, perhaps he was into prostitution, but to Ian's mind it was more likely to be blackmail. If so, the person, or persons, concerned would be able to sleep again at night. Unless, of course, they were foolish enough to allow it to happen again. One or the other, it did not matter now.

'Why does it always make you feel so full?' Moira asked, leaning back in her seat and holding her stomach.

'Not too full, I hope?'

She smiled, thinking Ian was in one of his more optimistic moods. After the strain of the case, what had happened with Lara, the long drive back and a filling meal she would hear his gentle snores before she had cleaned her teeth.